L.M. Merrington is an author, freelance writer and consultant. Her other books include a Gothic mystery, *Greythorne*, and a non-fiction communications handbook, *Communications for Volunteers: Low-Cost Strategies for Community Groups*. She lives in Australia with her husband, Tristan. For more information visit http://www.lmmerrington.com, or follow her on Facebook.

I0592504

the

IRON LINE

L.M. MERRINGTON

PAC BOOKS

First published by PAC Books in 2017
http://www.pacbooks.com.au

A catalogue record for this
book is available from the
National Library of Australia

ISBN: 9780648021568

Cover design by Raewyn Brack
Edited by Susan Cutsforth
Layout by Rachel Greene

For my parents, Amanda and Graeme.

CHAPTER 1

They call this the Train to Nowhere.

I couldn't remember where I'd first heard that—probably from some railway mate of Da's or Jim's—but as I stood on the platform watching the engine smoke and steam like a ravenous beast, it came back to me. For a second my certainty, which had stood me in good stead the past few months, wavered. I breathed deeply, staring back along the platform.

Beyond the near end lay the road into town; I could just see the rooftops ascending, terraced, up the hill, bathed in the golden light of late afternoon. Back there lay familiarity; people and places I'd known since birth, and who'd known me, for all the good it had done them. People who stopped and stared, and whispered behind their hands, who uttered polite pleasantries to my face and cast glances of sympathy—or disgust—when they thought I wasn't looking. Back there lay the only home I'd ever known; a home that would never be open to me again.

In the other direction, past the puffing engine, the rails stretched out into the unknown, a lone link to civilisation through the bush rising up around them. Out there was possibility—risk and danger, but also the chance of a new start. Out at the end of the line nobody knew me; I could be whoever and whatever I wanted. My heart thrilled at the thought. I turned my back on the town and hoisted myself into the carriage.

The smell of the train—furniture polish, old leather and soot—was comforting. I supposed I should feel more worry at leaving this place, but the lure of the land down the railway line was too strong. I'd always been one for wondering what lay round the bend, no matter how often Ma had told me curiosity killed the cat. Mind you, it had been that same curiosity that had got me involved with Jim in the first place, and look where that had landed me, so perhaps she had a point.

I shook my head to clear it of garbled thoughts of Jim and Ma and Da. None of that mattered now.

The train was a slow one, but I wasn't in any hurry. When the railway board had offered me a job manning the level crossing in Tungold, I had to ask where it was. It turned out to be a tiny town out at the end of the branch line. The railway was earmarked for expansion one of these days, but for now the miles of iron rails had to stop somewhere, and that place was

Tungold. But they got a mail train every day now, so what was once an isolated little outpost serving the farms roundabout was now something almost akin to civilisation, or so I'd been told. It would be a quiet life, I was sure, but it would be my own, and I hadn't had that for a long time.

It was the mail train I was going out on that afternoon, and I was the only passenger. After I tired of watching the bush go by, I wandered down to the mail carriage. It wasn't open to the public, but I knew the two lads who were busy sorting the letters that they picked up in the mailbags at each stop. We were like family out there on the railways.

"Hello, Tom," I said. He looked up, his face brightening. I called them 'lads', but Tom was nearly as old as my Da.

"Why, hello, young Jane," he said with a smile, but not stopping his sorting. "I was sorry to hear about your loss."

I shrugged and made a non-committal noise, trying to sound graceful, although I didn't know what to say. I was still shocked at how quickly I'd adjusted to life without Jim.

"They tell me you're bound for Tungold. Interesting choice of location, I must say."

"Not my choice. We go where duty sends us, isn't that right?" In truth, though, I was grateful for the job. With Jim dead I had nought to support myself, and I couldn't go back to Ma and Da, not after everything. But the railway took care of its own, and I wasn't the first widow to wind up as a gatekeeper out on the network, although at twenty-three I was likely one of the youngest. There were so few trains passing through Tungold that they probably didn't even really need a gatekeeper at all, but it was a way of helping loyal workers' widows while letting us maintain our dignity, and I appreciated it.

"Aye, that's right," Tom said, "but it's a queer town, I'll tell you that much."

"Queer in what way?"

His brow furrowed. "Can't put me finger on it—never spent a great deal of time there, you know—but it's just odd, unfriendly like."

"They don't like strangers," young Mack chimed in.

"Aren't all small towns like that?" I'd never lived in a really small country town, although Goulburn had felt that way sometimes.

Mack chewed his lip. "Nah," he said finally. "Most of the places we go are glad to see us. Can't get enough of the railway or railway folk. But them Tungold locals—they look at you like you're planning to murder their mothers. Tom's right, it's a queer place."

"I'm sure it's different if you live there and get to know them." I tried to sound optimistic, because at that point I had to be.

"Aye, mebbe," Mack said, although he didn't seem convinced. Tom just shrugged.

"Sorry, lass," he said distractedly, "but we gotta get these letters sorted before the next stop or our lives won't be worth living. Best of luck to you."

"And you. We may meet in Tungold one of these days."

"I daresay we will, that." He turned back to his letters and I took the hint and returned to my carriage, feeling inexplicably restless. I settled into my seat and stared out the window as the engine began to chug and puff its way up a hill, slowing almost to walking pace. The light was beginning to fade, but it was January—high summer—and it wouldn't be properly dark for another few hours yet. Lottie had begged me not to leave before Christmas, so just for her I'd waited until the New Year, not that it really made that much of a difference. I still spent Christmas alone. But I was glad she'd at least heeded me when I told her not to see me off. If she'd been there I may not have had the courage to go.

The scenery outside was typical bush country—all grey-green and brown and gold, the hills jagged and unforgiving, with clumps of sandstone poking through the brush like knees through a threadbare quilt. It was quite a contrast to the 'old country', or so I'd been told. Although I'd never been there, I'd heard about it often enough from Ma, for I think in her heart she'd never really left it, despite being settled here nearly thirty years. She'd talk of the rolling emerald hills—at which point Da would interject that the only reason they were so blooming green was because it rained all the sodding time—and the ancient little villages with their stone churches so old that the very saints had set foot in them, not like here where nothing was old and everything was rough and brown, except the sky, which blazed so blue you feared it'd fry you like an egg. Da would just laugh, eyes twinkling like a leprechaun's. He didn't have much time for the old country—for they'd arrested and transported him for stealing when he wasn't much more than a lad, and after he'd won his freedom he'd made himself a new life, doing fencing and droving and all sorts of odd jobs as needed doing, and then labouring on the railways when they came. But Ma was the child of free settlers, come over from Ireland when she was just a girl, and she never really took to the place. I asked her once why she hadn't just gone back to the old country once she was grown, and she told me that she'd considered it, but she'd had the misfortune to meet a cheeky lad at just the wrong time—she made eyes at

Da as she said this—and so found herself as a wife and mother down in southern New South Wales.

Thinking about Ma and Da made my chest ache, so I stopped. I wondered if they'd heard I was headed to Tungold. Lottie might have told them. I told myself that maybe I'd write to them when I got there, even though I knew I probably wouldn't—I hadn't managed to yet.

I leaned my head against the window frame and let my mind wander, and before I knew it I'd drifted into a doze, only to jerk awake periodically when the train stopped at the various small towns along the way. The world outside had grown dark, the swinging carriage lamps the only illumination, reflecting my image back to me in the smudged window glass.

I'd lost count of how many hours we'd been travelling when the guard came through calling, "Last stop Tungold! All off for Tungold!" as if I weren't the only passenger.

"You made it," he said with a grin, and I wondered if there had been any doubt of it. "Don't worry, you can always get another train home if it proves too much for you, being stuck way out here in the middle of bloody nowhere." He chuckled as if he'd made some sort of joke, but I just stared at him stonily. It was late and my mind felt thick and stupid, my neck stiff from sleeping in the train.

"I'm sure I'll be fine, thank you."

"Yeah, well, you're braver than me. This place gives me the willies. You could bowl a bloody cricket ball down what they call the main street and not hit anybody. I likes me towns a bit more civilised, thank you very much." He stuck his finger in his ear and wiggled it round distractedly, before inspecting the result and wiping it on his trousers. My eyebrows rose. Turning away, I looked out the window again as the train crossed a road, the white level crossing gates shut, then slowed and drew into Tungold station.

I suppose I'd been spoilt by Goulburn's grand station, with its terracotta-red brick, arched windows and numerous platforms, but Tungold station struck me as little more than a glorified cottage. In the light of the lamps strung along the platform, I could see that it was built of cream-coloured weatherboards, with a red corrugated iron roof, out of which two brick chimneys peeked. The verandah extended out over the platform to provide a modicum of shelter for passengers unlucky enough to be caught there on rainy days. To the left of the station, looking from the track, stood a large white wooden sign, proclaiming 'TUNGOLD' in big black letters. Behind it, a white picket fence extended to keep a patch of garden—or weeds, at least—from encroaching on the platform. The platform itself didn't so much end as peter out, sloping down to the road. The station's paint was peeling and the whole place had an air of neglect. I wondered what I'd let myself in for.

The train pulled in and ground to a halt. I collected my bag and stepped down, surveying my surroundings. I had a trunk in the luggage van and I wondered what my chances were of finding a porter. The place seemed deserted, save for the lads from the train unloading the mail and other goods. I stood watching as the locomotive was uncoupled and run back along a short second line to the other end of the train, all ready to depart. The train would stay for maybe an hour and then off it would go, back to the outside world, leaving me here all alone in this strange place. For a second it was all I could do not to jump back into the carriage, but I took a deep breath and forced myself to stand firm. I walked down the platform to where the luggage was being unloaded and located my trunk, looking around for a porter, but none materialised.

Eventually the guard noticed me standing there and took pity on me.

"You won't find anyone to help you tonight, I'll be bound," he shrugged. "Best go along and come back tomorrow. I'll see your trunk's put away safe."

I bit my lip, but there weren't many other options. It was lucky I'd thought to put a change of nightclothes and underthings in my travelling bag.

"Thank you. I don't suppose you know where the gatekeeper's cottage is?"

He looked at me like I was simple. "Next to the level crossing, of course. We passed it as we came in." He gestured vaguely back up the line. "Check under the mat for a key. They don't care much for security round here. Think that locking your door means you've got something to hide." He guffawed, but I couldn't manage more than a tight smile, and he turned away in apparent disgust. He clearly wanted nothing more to do with me.

Fighting off a sudden wave of wretchedness that threatened to overwhelm me, I raised my head high and set off down the platform towards the level crossing. I had no lantern, but thankfully the moon was bright and I could find my way without too much difficulty along the road that ran parallel to the railway line.

Up ahead I saw another road, larger this time, which crossed both my street and the railway line. Next to the level crossing, jammed between the roads and the line, stood a small white cottage, not dissimilar in design to the station.

I walked around to the front of the cottage, which was bounded by a rickety white picket fence on three sides and the railway line on the fourth. In the moonlight I saw a pale dirt path overgrown with weeds and bushes that had sought to reclaim their own. The gate, when I tried to open it, screeched pitifully and stubbornly resisted until I kicked it, then opened so swiftly that I stumbled through. Dead leaves and twigs crackled under my boots as I picked my way gingerly along the path. Judging by the state of the garden, the cottage hadn't been lived in for some time, and its windows stared out at me balefully, black and cold, like the eyes of some long-dead animal. I shivered, although the night was warm.

Climbing the three creaking stairs to the verandah, I reached under the ratty doormat and sighed with relief when my hand encountered cold metal. I withdrew a large brass key and slipped it into the lock on the door. It resisted my attempts to turn it and I felt despair welling up in my chest until, just as it seemed hopeless, the lock clicked and the knob turned under my fingers. I stepped over the threshold into a dark, musty-smelling hallway, illuminated only by the stray strands of moonlight from the doorway. A rush of cold, damp air surged forth to greet me, and clouds of dust billowed around my ankles.

A terrible screeching rent the air, sending my heart pounding and making me gasp. By the time I realised it was only possums fighting somewhere in the nearby bush, my hands were shaking. I pressed them to my face and forced myself to laugh at the situation, although it came out more like a sob.

"Welcome home."

CHAPTER 2

The morning light woke me, and for a second I struggled to remember where I was. I sat up and looked around, blinking groggily, the wrought iron bedstead groaning in protest. Dust motes floated in a shaft of sunlight, which had managed to pierce through the creeper that all but covered the window.

Gradually it all came back to me. After I'd recovered from my shock at the possums the previous night, I'd fumbled my way into the house, aided by nothing but the moonlight. One hand pressed to the hallway wall, I'd picked my way gingerly towards the back of the cottage, where I assumed the kitchen would be, hoping I wouldn't encounter any obstacles that might cause me to fall and break my head. I managed it eventually, despite a heart-stopping moment when I stumbled down a low step at the end of the hall. The kitchen was brighter, with moonlight streaming in through two sets of windows, and I was able to see just enough to find a candle stub on the mantelpiece and—thankfully—a half-empty box of matches next to it. By that stage I was feeling utterly wretched, so I only explored long enough to unearth the bedroom. I nearly cried when I saw that the bed was unmade, with only a moth-eaten old blanket folded at its foot, but in the end there was nothing for it but to undress, curl up on the rather stained mattress, pull the musty-smelling blanket up to my chin and sleep as best I could.

It was deep night when I was woken by the rattling and clattering of a train. I ran to the window but could see nothing in the gloom. My next thought was one of panic—I hadn't closed the level crossing gates!—but the danger was over before I really had time to comprehend it. I crawled back into my rough bed, consoling myself that there was unlikely to be much traffic in the dead of night and the risk of an accident was low. But my heart was racing and I found sleep elusive. I'd understood that Tungold had only one train a day; no one had mentioned anything about a late-night run. But the train had been unmistakable, so what was going on? I chewed over the conundrum for what felt like hours, without success, eventually falling into a fitful doze. When I woke, groggy and tired, I couldn't say for sure that it hadn't been a dream.

Consequently, I wasn't in the most congenial of moods, but the day outside was sunny and cheerful, and it was already warm. It would probably be scorching by mid-afternoon.

I dressed in the previous day's clothes—for everything else was in my trunk at the station—then headed down to the kitchen, poking my head into rooms as I went, dust billowing around my ankles. The house was a typical worker's cottage, with rooms opening off a central hallway. Opposite the bedroom was the sitting room, then towards the back were the kitchen and the laundry. The verandah wrapped all around the house from front to back, and beyond that, away through the jungle of a garden, was the outhouse. I looked at the tangle of weeds, thinking with a shudder of all the snakes and spiders that could be lurking in there. It was only necessity that got me out into the wilderness, and I jumped at every rustle in the undergrowth. When I opened the outhouse door, small black-and-red spiders scuttled away from the sudden light.

On the way back, I stopped at the pump to splash some water on my face, for in spite of the sturdy ceramic sink in the kitchen, running water had clearly not yet made it to my corner of Tungold. I climbed the stairs to the verandah and stood there, surveying my patch of jungle and the bush beyond it, wondering what to do next. My usual decisiveness seemed to have deserted me.

Eventually I decided that I should first fetch my trunk from the station. And somewhere in there, I supposed, I should also do my job, whatever that entailed. I hoped someone at the station would be able to enlighten me.

If anything, the station looked more pitiful in daylight than it had in darkness, its peeling paint clearly visible. The railway yard was small as these things went, with a similar air of benign neglect. I noticed another modest weatherboard building across the other side of the tracks that I must have missed last night—I assumed it was the barracks for the railwaymen who did the late mail run and sometimes stopped the night.

As I walked up the platform I spied two men deep in conversation. The first was the stationmaster, judging by the uniform, while his companion, who had his back to me, looked like some sort of gentleman or official. They were debating each other with some intensity, and I was reluctant to interrupt, so I stood awkwardly under the shade of the verandah, shifting my weight from one foot to the other, hoping that sooner or later they'd notice me. It took some time, but eventually I caught the stationmaster's eye and he nodded to me over his companion's shoulder. The other man turned around, and my heart started beating so fast I was afraid it might spring out of my chest. The mean, piggy little eyes in the fleshy red face, the shock of black hair; they were all familiar to me, and I could see by the little start he gave that he recognised me too. He said something to the stationmaster, then the two men shook hands and he strode off down the platform in the opposite direction to where I was standing.

The stationmaster watched him go for a moment then turned back to me. He walked over, looking me up and down warily, clearly trying to figure out who I was.

"Mrs Adams?" he asked at last. He must have be getting close to retirement age, for his hair and moustache were peppered with grey, and his face lined from what I took to be many years of manning a station in all weather.

"Yes."

"George Bailey, stationmaster."

"Pleased to meet you, sir."

"So you're the new gatekeeper, then. Only the second time we've had a woman working the railway out here. Don't even have tea ladies." He sniffed. "First Lily and now you. We seem to be making a habit of it. Still, it saves me from having to do the gates myself, so that's a blessing, I suppose."

I wasn't quite sure what to make of this odd little man, so I said nothing. He was like no stationmaster I'd ever met, and I'd met a few over the years. They'd ranged from taciturn to kindly, but they were all highly professional and competent, and didn't run off at the mouth as Mr Bailey seemed inclined to do. It was probably no wonder he was overseeing a shack out in Tungold and not a major station elsewhere, but I kept this thought to myself.

"And what can I do for you?" he asked, breaking a slightly uncomfortable silence. I tried to stop my brow crinkling in surprise, because I would have thought it was obvious.

"Uh...I came to discuss the particulars of my job, sir. I haven't been given any guidance about when I should start or exactly what the role entails," I said, treading carefully.

"Oh yes, quite, quite. You'd best come into my office, then."

There were only two doors in the tiny station building: one marked 'Stationmaster' and the other 'Storage'. He seemed to be having trouble with the key to his office; he rattled it ineffectually in the lock, then withdrew it, spat on it and tried again.

"I also left my trunk here last night," I added, to fill the silence. "There was no porter when I arrived."

"Indeed. Well, I'm sure we can see to it." He wrenched the key violently, which worked; the door burst open so suddenly he almost tumbled through it. I wondered if he'd been drinking, for he seemed tired and out of sorts.

The office was tiny, with just a desk piled high with papers, a single chair opposite and a small bookcase filled with dusty back-copies of the *New South Wales Railway Budget*. A small fireplace was the only comforting thing about it.

"Right, the level crossing," he muttered, waving me to the chair and placing himself behind the desk. "It's pretty straightforward, really. You've found the telephone?" I stared at him blankly and he clicked his tongue in exasperation. "The telephone—in your cottage. Beside the front door."

"I must have missed it, sir. Apologies."

He waved my excuse away. "You'll get a telephone call when the train departs Merrin Vale. It's an hour between there and here so you'll know when to expect the train. This is the timetable. But be sure to wait for the call regardless, in case the train is delayed." He pushed a rather crumpled piece of paper across the desk to me. As I'd thought, there was only the one mail train per day—in the evening, the same one I'd come out on—and no specific passenger services. My workload was going to be rather light.

"I'm sorry sir, but are these the only trains?"

"What? Yes, of course. Definitely the only trains!" He seemed strangely defensive about what I'd thought was a fairly simple question. He stood up and took a pipe from the mantelpiece, knocking it out with some agitation and then refilling it from a tobacco tin he found in his desk drawer.

"Anything else?" he asked, puffing away.

"Can you tell me about my predecessor—Lily, was it? Why did she leave the post?" I didn't really know why I was interested; I was just making conversation. But at the mention of her name he started visibly.

"Lily…well, she…passed away. Quite recently. Heart trouble. Very sudden. Poor woman, it was quite the tragedy."

"Oh, I'm sorry." That certainly wasn't what I'd been expecting.

A painful silence fell, and I wondered if I had to wait to be dismissed. But something about the timetable was still niggling at me.

"Forgive me, sir, but I'm still not clear about the schedule. It's just that last night I could have sworn I heard a train go past very late, at perhaps two or three o'clock, but there's no mention of such a service on here."

Mr Bailey looked troubled; he bit his lip, causing his moustache to waffle up and down like some sort of fussy animal. He sighed and sat back down, looking suddenly old. "Some people would say I shouldn't be telling you this, Mrs Adams," he said. "Give our town a bad reputation and all that. But the truth is, Tungold is haunted."

This was so unexpected that I nearly laughed out loud, and I had to strive to keep a neutral expression. I didn't believe in ghosts—not the spectral kind, at least, although the kind we created for ourselves were a whole other matter—and it seemed ridiculous to hear a man of Mr Bailey's age and position talking about them with such apparent credence.

"Haunted? Really?" I tried to keep the scepticism out of my voice.

"Oh yes. There's a ghost train. It runs along here sometimes in the dead of night. It rattles and crashes just like a real train, but it has an eerie glow about it, and there's no one driving it. It pulls a single carriage, filled with the souls of sinners on their way to hell, it's said."

"Surely not!"

He nodded seriously, and I got the feeling he was enjoying it. "Back when the railway first came to Tungold, there was a terrible accident," he said. "The line originally ran through the town to a small station near a prospecting camp down the escarpment. One day a train pulling a carriage of miners and their families lost its brakes on the hill and derailed. Everyone on board was killed, but they haven't been able to rest quiet. And now the authorities are talking of reopening and extending the line again. Mark my words, it'll be a black day when they do. All them poor souls won't stand for it."

"And you've seen this train with your own eyes?"

"I certainly have, and I'm not the only one. A number of us have seen and heard it—from the safety of our windows of course. But poor Lily couldn't contain herself, and her curiosity was the death of her." He shook his head in apparent sorrow. "I understand she heard it go by one night and went outside to take a closer look, but her heart couldn't stand the fright of it and she dropped down dead where she stood. You mark my words, if you hear the ghost train go by, you put your head under the covers and stay there till it's gone. Them that encounter it up close pay the price."

I didn't know what to say, so I just stared at him rather gormlessly. He puffed away on his pipe for a minute, then said, "So, anything else? You'll be paid once a month, same as the rest of the railway staff. You know the rate, I take it?"

The transition was so abrupt that it left me rather thrown, but I nodded, because I'd discussed this in Goulburn before I left. I certainly wouldn't be rich, but I'd have more than enough to live on, and it was a decent wage considering the relatively little work I actually had to do.

"Well then, if that's all..."

I stood up at this obvious dismissal, my head still spinning. "Yes, thank you, sir. I just need to collect my trunk."

"Of course." Mr Bailey saw me to the door, then bellowed, "Stanley!", making me jump. At the summons, a gangly youth appeared, wheeling a decrepit old trolley. His uniform, although standard issue, was creased and smudged, the brass buttons unpolished. He would never get away with that in Goulburn, I thought, remembering the old stationmaster there and how he'd drilled the staff with military precision.

"This is Mrs Adams, the new gatekeeper," Mr Bailey said. "She needs her trunk taking to the cottage."

"Very good, sir." Stanley opened the storage door and ducked inside, emerging with my trunk. The trolley creaked and complained when he loaded the trunk onto it, but it held up.

As we walked back towards my cottage I couldn't get Mr Bailey's story out of my head. It seemed utterly fanciful, a cautionary tale made up to scare children, but he didn't seem the kind of man who would have an imagination inventive enough to concoct such a fantasy. I wondered if Stanley had heard of the mysterious glowing locomotive, or whether the poor stationmaster had just been spending too much time alone with his trains.

"May I ask you something, Stanley?"

"Mm-hmm."

"I've heard there's a ghost train that runs along here at night. Do you know of it?"

Stanley took so long to respond that I wondered if he'd understood the question, but then he just shrugged.

"Dunno."

"So you've never seen it?"

"Nah."

It was as I thought, then—the poor stationmaster was touched in the head.

"Me sister's seen it, though."

"Really?"

"Well, she said she woke up one night and saw a glow. But I dunno. Polly's not that bright." As we reached the garden gate, I reflected that this appeared to be a family trait.

Stanley carried the trunk inside, unloaded it at the foot of the bed and looked at me expectantly. I dug in my purse for a coin, which clearly wasn't as much as he was hoping for, because he seemed slightly affronted, but I held firm.

"Nice to meet you," he said, heading for the door, in a tone that indicated he thought it was anything but. After he'd gone, I sat on the bed and rested my head in my hands to ease the pounding that was beginning behind my eyes. What had I done?

CHAPTER 3

I spent the rest of the morning and most of the afternoon unpacking and cleaning. Thankfully the house had all the basic implements, so I did the best I could to sweep away the months of dust and dead insects that had accumulated since Lily's death. Despite the heat, I opened up the windows and doors to let the gusty northerly breeze—bushfire weather—blow through. I found linens in a cupboard in my bedroom, but they were soiled and stained at the folds, so I scrubbed them in the copper until my hands were raw, then hung them on the verandah to dry. The good thing about this weather was that washing dried fast, although I had a devil of a time trying to keep the dust from the roadway from blowing onto the sheets and turning into little spots of mud on the wet cotton. By five o'clock I was completely tuckered out, but I also felt a swelling sense of pride and achievement as I surveyed my now spotless little cottage. Perhaps I really could make a go of it here.

It was only as I was lounging in the old rocking chair on the verandah, sweat streaming from my brow, that I realised I had no food in the house. There was chopped wood for the stove tucked away in a dry spot under the back verandah, and pots in the cupboard, but with nothing to put in them they were useless to me. I sighed. My body ached and I was starting to feel the effects of my long journey and the previous night's broken sleep. But there was nothing for it—I had to go into town and see if I could purchase at least some basic provisions.

I had a quick wash, smartened myself up and left the cottage, pulling the door behind me and locking it out of habit. Outside my gate, I stood at the junction for a moment then turned left, away from the railway line, down what looked to be the main street. A worn, faded sign reading 'Welcome to Tungold' hung crookedly from its post, weeds sprouting around its base. The road at least was well-kept, smooth and flat with only the odd pothole. There was no one in sight, but as I walked I heard the thud of a horse's hooves and the crunch of wheels coming up behind me. I stepped to the side of the road and watched as a cart pulled by a bay horse trundled by. It was driven by a stocky man of about forty, with mid-brown hair and small grey eyes, who turned to stare unsmilingly at me as he went past, swivelling in his seat and watching me even as the cart disappeared into the distance. I shook my head—even in Goulburn a driver passing a woman walking alone would most likely have offered a lift. I muttered to myself about country hospitality and continued on, keeping to the verge in case there was any more traffic, but

I reached the town centre, such as it was, without seeing another soul.

A collection of necessary shops was strung out along the main street—butcher, greengrocer, apothecary, baker, general store and a small tea room— but, to my dismay, all were closed for the evening. The wind blew dust eddies desolately down the road and whistled under the eaves of the stores. The only building with any sign of life was a double-storey stone edifice with 'Tungold Hotel' painted on its frontage in large letters. It was a typical country public house, with a wide verandah running along all sides on the ground floor and a balcony on the second, the latter bound with iron lace facings. Cast-iron support posts extended at intervals from the red tin roof down to the verandah. The cart that had passed me was parked out the front, along with several horses tied to hitching posts. For a moment I stood dithering in the road, but there was really nothing for it. I stepped over the large gutter onto the hotel's verandah, for this place seemed to be my only hope of getting a hot meal this evening. Taking a deep breath, I pushed open the door.

Inside it was cool and dim, with wells of golden lamplight reflecting off dark polished wood and brass fittings. The bar was elaborately carved from red cedar, its rows of glasses and bottles shining like jewels. The door creaked loudly as I entered, and every head in the place turned to stare at me. There were no other women present except a single young barmaid, and even she couldn't seem to pull her gaze away from my face. I stood there like a fool, not knowing what to say. The truth was, I'd never been in a pub before. Ma had had a moral objection to young ladies drinking, and there'd been plenty of times I'd got a second-hand dose of alcohol's effects after Jim had had a big night. It had almost been enough to make me want to join the Temperance League, although I was hardly one for strict moral standards, as Ma would no doubt attest.

The strange tableau was broken by the arrival of another woman, this one of middling years and generous proportions, bustling in from somewhere behind the bar.

"Can I help you?"

"I was hoping for a meal."

"We don't serve ladies."

"Not even food? I won't be drinking."

"Them's the rules."

I bristled. "But that's ridiculous. I'd like to speak to the proprietor, please."

"I *am* the proprietor. Annie Graham's my name, and what I say goes."

"Well, I never..."

"Now then, Miss, you're causing a scene. If you wouldn't mind just stepping outside..." She was right—all the drinkers, clearly starved of excitement, were staring avidly at us, lined up like a bunch of galahs on a telegraph wire. I wanted to yell at them to mind their own business, but I suspected that would be less than prudent.

Annie Graham was shepherding me towards the door when it opened in a gust of furnace-like air, and a sandy-haired young man in a policeman's uniform stepped through.

"Good evening, Mrs Graham," he said, catching sight of us. "I'm here for dinner, if you please."

"Evening, Constable," she replied. "Polly will take care of you. I've just got some business to attend to. Now, Miss," she muttered, turning back to me, "if you just go quietly, we'll none of us have to make a fuss."

"It's 'Mrs'," I hissed, giving her the most cutting stare I could muster. "Mrs Jane Adams. And I will *not* go quietly." I knew many pubs wouldn't serve women, but I never could abide bullies.

"Is everything all right?" the constable asked.

Annie Graham turned back to him with a huge, rather false smile. "Everything's fine," she said. "This young lady was just leaving."

"I was only seeking a meal," I blurted out.

"Really?" The policeman furrowed his brow. He had an open, friendly face—so different from the others I'd met so far in this town—and twinkling blue eyes, but there was a hardness there too, which I supposed came with the job. "I don't see why that should be a problem." He turned a questioning gaze on Mrs Graham.

"But you know the rules about ladies in hotel establishments as well as I do, Constable," she said, rather defensively. "I'm just enforcing them, is all."

"Well, really, Mrs Graham, I think we could make an exception," the policeman said reasonably. "While many see the sense in banning women from the public bar for their own moral safety, I doubt even the Temperance League could object to a lady having a meal in the back dining room. I'm sure she would be perfectly safe there. In fact, I'll even invite her to be my dining companion to make sure. I trust that will allay your objections?"

Mrs Graham's expression was thunderous, and I wondered if she was going to argue, but after a moment's thought she relented. "Very well," she said, then gestured to the barmaid. "Table for two," she said. The girl led us into a rear dining room, away from the prying eyes of the clientele, but I could feel their gazes boring into my back as I went.

The young constable pulled out a chair for me, and I sat, wondering at the situation. While I was grateful that I no longer had to go hungry, I had mixed feelings about being rescued in such a fashion. Once upon a time, I would have been bowled over by such chivalry, but these days I was suspicious of it, because I'd learned that nothing came for free.

But he smiled kindly at me as he sat down, and in spite of myself I noticed he had a dimple in one cheek. "I don't believe we've met—at least not properly," he said. "I'm Alec Ward."

"Jane Adams. Pleased to meet you. And thank you for your help."

"Any time. The locals can be a bit...overzealous...sometimes. Are you new in town?"

"Very—I just arrived last night."

"Well, it's nice to meet another recent arrival. I've only been here three months myself, and there are still people I don't know."

I sipped my glass of water, unsure how to respond.

"So what brings you to Tungold?" he asked.

"I'm the new level crossing gatekeeper on the railway."

"Really? Interesting. You're Lily's replacement, then?"

"Yes, I suppose I am." I paused, wondering how much to discuss, then threw caution to the wind. "I heard she passed away."

"Yes, she did, quite unexpectedly one night. They found her outside her house, beside the railway tracks. It was my first case here—I'd only been in town a week."

"That must have been a shock."

"It was the strangest thing, you know. There wasn't a mark on her, but she had this look of sheer terror on her face. I've never seen anything like it. I wanted to conduct an investigation, but Doctor Carter swore she died of natural causes, so there was nothing to investigate."

"You think she was murdered?" It sounded like something out of the plot of a penny dreadful.

He shrugged, shaking his head. "I doubt it. According to the doctor, she'd been having trouble with her heart for a while and it just gave up on her. Although I do wonder what she was doing on the railway line in the middle of the night." He shrugged again, then grinned. "This is a small town and not much happens here, so when something unusual comes up, one's imagination tends to run riot."

I was about to ask him about the ghost train, but we were interrupted by Polly bringing our dinner. "Anything else, Mrs Adams?" she asked as she set the plate of stew in front of me. Her tone contained none of the acid I expected; she sounded simply bored.

"No, thank you."

"I didn't realise you were married," Alec said as she left, and I knew he was thinking I looked too young. "Is your husband working out here too?"

I shook my head. "I'm a widow. My husband passed away about a year-and-a-half ago." Technically I was still in mourning, but I'd taken to wearing grey and brown rather than black. I couldn't stand widow's weeds; I didn't want to remember.

"Oh, my condolences."

I smiled in that way I'd learned to whenever anyone said anything nice about Jim or implied how much I must miss him, but I couldn't help feeling a bit disingenuous. "He was a railway worker and was killed in an accident; he fell under a train. The railway board offered me this job to help me earn a living after he died." The silence that followed was discomforting, so I changed the subject.

"I hope you don't mind my asking, but why don't you eat with the men in the bar rather than out here by yourself? I mean, apart from chaperoning me, of course." He smiled sunnily again as if I'd made a joke. He looked far too light-hearted to be a policeman.

"I do, most of the time," he said. "But I'm new in town, and the face of the law; it makes people a bit uncomfortable to have me around. So sometimes I prefer to dine alone, present company excepted, of course."

"Of course." I thought of those hard, staring eyes in the bar and could hardly blame him. "How long have you been a policeman?"

"Going on seven years. My dad was a sergeant in Berrima and it's all I've ever wanted to do, so I joined as soon as I was old enough."

"Tungold seems a strange choice of posting."

"You're rather frank, aren't you?" he said with a laugh, and I blushed. I knew I was overly blunt. I'd have said it was my Irish blood, although Ma would have contended that it was simply beyond all human efforts to make a lady of me so she eventually gave up.

"Truth is," he continued, "this wasn't a choice for me. They needed someone out here when Constable Jenkins retired and I got landed with it." There was something in the way he said it that made me think there was more to this story than he was letting on, but I let it pass. I had no doubt I'd be seeing more of the handsome young constable, small as this town was, and I'd get it out of him eventually.

We'd finished our stew by now, and Polly returned to clear the plates and bring the bill. I reached for my purse, but he stopped me, insisting on paying for mine as well. I wasn't so flush with cash that I could refuse a free meal, so I let him. If Polly had thoughts on this she didn't air them, but I had no doubt the gossip would be all over town by morning.

The stares as we walked out through the bar were even starker than when I entered, and I could almost read their owners' minds. Annie Graham was polishing glasses behind the bar, and her gaze as she looked at me was icy. I wondered if I'd inadvertently cast myself as the town hussy. I was suddenly thankful there were no other women there, for to them I'd surely be the young widow come to town to steal their husbands, as if I'd want any of this half-shaven rabble of labourers and drunks. I wondered if Constable Ward had noticed the chill in the room, but if he had he gave no sign of it.

"May I walk you home?" he asked as we stood on the pub verandah in the twilight. I hesitated, for the trouble with Jim had begun just this way, back when I was only sixteen.

"You think I'll get lost between here and my door?"

"Not a bit of it. But the road is dark and...well, even small country towns aren't completely safe."

"Do all policemen suffer such worries, or just where young women are concerned?"

"In truth? I'm just enjoying conversing with someone who isn't a drunken lout."

"Thank you...I think," I said, smiling wryly and stepping off the verandah. "Come on then. You may walk me home, if only because you're so free with your compliments."

As much as I hated to admit it, there was something a little thrilling about walking in the moonlight with a handsome policeman. Having married Jim so young, I felt I'd missed my share of courting. And Constable Ward seemed like a gentleman; he kept a respectful distance between us, and his banter was light and friendly without being overly familiar, not like Jim who, right from the start, made it clear that what he most desired was to take a tumble with me. Even so, I was wary, because I'd learned the hard way that, no matter how much you think you know someone, you can still be terribly, terribly wrong. So I farewelled Constable Ward at the garden gate with nothing more than a wave, but all the same, I couldn't help feeling that life in Tungold might not be as dull as I'd envisioned.

CHAPTER 4

I confess that, upon arriving home, I was in a bit of a girlish daze. The night was still warm, so I sat out on the verandah for a while, enjoying the eucalyptus-scented dusk. It was so peaceful that I drifted into a sort of trance, letting my mind wander through pleasant daydreams in which a handsome young constable featured rather prominently, much as I tried to banish him.

I was jerked suddenly from my reverie by the thrum and screech of the railway tracks beside the house. I scrambled to my feet in horror, trying to recall Mr Bailey's timetable, for I hadn't heard the telephone, if in fact it had rung at all. I dashed down the verandah steps and up the path, almost wrenching the garden gate off its hinges in my haste, and ran to the level crossing, my breath gasping painfully in my chest. I could see the lights of the locomotive bearing down and, worse, a horse and cart coming fast—heedlessly fast—up the road from town.

For a second I felt paralysed with indecision, but there was no time. I skipped across the tracks and pulled the far gate into place, then hurried back and fixed the second gate, feeling it slam shut with a satisfying thud. I wasn't a moment too soon. Just as the gate closed, the train rumbled through—slowing, but still going fast enough to kill anyone unlucky enough to get caught in its path. The driver gestured at me out the side of the cabin, and although I couldn't hear his words over the shriek of metal, I knew he was asking what the bloody hell I was playing at.

I turned around at a cry of, "Whoa, there!" as the cart that had been barrelling up the road skidded to a stop just short of the gates. The driver was the same man who had passed me earlier, and he fixed me with the same stony stare. He said nothing, but he didn't have to—his contempt was clear, and his gaze never left me until I reopened the gates and he went on his way.

It wasn't until I returned home that the full enormity of the situation hit me. The cart driver's contempt for me had nothing on what I felt for myself, for I'd always prided myself on working to the highest standards. The shame sat like a rock on my chest, alongside a gnawing anxiety about what the morrow would bring when Mr Bailey found out, as he surely would. In despair I went to bed, weeping into my pillow until I fell into an uneasy sleep.

I didn't have to wait long for the summons to arrive the next morning: Stanley was at my door first thing. "Mr Bailey wants to see ya," he said, not even trying to hide his smirk. I put on my hat and walked down to the station with my head held high, not wanting to give him the satisfaction of seeing my true feelings.

"Come in," Mr Bailey called in answer to my knock, and I tentatively pushed open the door.

"Not a good start, was it, Mrs Adams?" he said with no preamble. He didn't invite me to sit, so I stayed standing, staring at my boots.

"No, sir."

"Even after I expressly instructed you on how to conduct your work. Can you offer any explanation?"

"I...I didn't hear the telephone, sir."

"And why not? Merrin Vale assures me they called you."

It would be so easy to lie, to blame it on faulty wiring. "I was out."

"*Out?*"

"Yes, sir. I went into town to purchase some food."

"And you were tardy returning, even though you would have seen on the timetable that the train was due?"

There was really nothing to say to this, so I simply nodded. Whether I was late returning or just plain forgot, it was all the same in the end.

"Heh. Well, perhaps a predilection for hard work is too much to expect from a young girl such as yourself. I have to say, I was concerned when they told me your age. I've always thought that a woman doesn't grow out of her flighty tendencies until at least forty, and sometimes not even then."

I seethed at this—many of his male engine drivers and other workers were my age or younger, and he wouldn't dream of saying the same thing about them—and if there had been less at stake I'd have given him a piece of my mind. But as it was, I was forced to stare at a knot in the floorboards and endure the slander.

"I hope you understand the gravity of your actions, young woman. You could have caused the serious injury or death of a number of people, not to mention untold damage to the railway infrastructure. I could report you and have you removed from your post."

"Yes, sir." I knew he could, but there was no point begging. In my experience, it had never stopped a man from doing whatever he wanted to in the end.

"But I won't, in this instance, seeing as no accident actually occurred. Although rest assured, if it happens again you'll be out on your ear, do you understand? I'll be keeping a close eye on you."

"Yes, sir. It won't happen again."

"Good. That's all...for now."

"Thank you, sir." I scurried out, glad to be back in the fresh air. I was thankful that I'd got away with nothing more than a stern warning, but the shame of the situation still gnawed at me. This was meant to be a new start in a new place where, in time, I might even grow to be respected and admired. Instead, I'd nearly caused an horrific accident, and no doubt the story would be all over town by supper time, if it wasn't already. Maybe I'd never fit in here, because maybe the problem was *me*. Ma had always said I wouldn't amount to anything, and perhaps she was right.

It took all my courage to ready myself to walk into town. Even as I made a shopping list and collected my basket, I wished I could simply lock all the doors, crawl into my bed and hide from the world. I'd experienced my fair share of humiliation over the years, but it never seemed to get any easier.

An examination of the pantry, however, revealed a dire situation. If I wanted to eat that evening—and I didn't feel I could show my face in the pub again, not after last night—then I had to go shopping. I sighed. Needs must, as Ma would say.

I saw not a single soul on the road into town; as the train guard had said, you could bowl a cricket ball clean down the main street without hitting anyone. I wondered where they all lived. There must be people somewhere, else why bother with a town at all? There were certainly quite a few of them in the pub last night. Maybe they only came out after dark.

Still, it was a beautiful summer morning, one of those golden days where the temperature was perfect, with just a light breeze, and the sky seemed to shimmer. There were still several months left of scorching days and sticky, sleepless nights, where the grass crackled underfoot and everyone was on edge, alert to the smell of smoke, and this was a welcome respite.

Despite the glorious weather, I walked like one marching to my doom, for I knew not what I'd encounter in town. I tried to convince myself that I was overreacting, and that it would take more than a simple mistake to permanently tarnish my reputation. To the people of Tungold, I was whoever I told them I was. I was simply a young widow looking for a new start, and anything more than that was immaterial, because I liked to think that all sins could be forgiven.

It was too early for the pub to be open, and the hitching posts out the front were deserted, but glancing up at the balcony I saw Polly beating a rug. I raised my hand in greeting, but she either didn't recognise me or pretended not to, for she just stared right through me. I shrugged to myself. It meant nothing.

There seemed to be a bit more life further into town, with a few people going in and out of the shops. The stores were fairly primitive compared to Goulburn, just weatherboard and slab huts with their signs painted above the verandahs in big, bold letters. There were a few carts parked outside, and enough people around—even if it was only half a dozen or so—that it seemed like a bustling marketplace compared to what I'd seen so far.

A clutch of women was milling outside Smith & Son, Grocery and Drapery—the first I'd seen in town apart from Polly and Annie. I took it that the morning shop was also a social hour, for there seemed to be some animated gossip going on. But the idle chatter stopped abruptly when they caught sight of me, as if a tap had been turned off. I should have been getting used to hostile stares by now, but it still unnerved me more than I'd care to admit. I took a deep breath.

"Good morning," I said brightly to hide my discomfort, but no one returned my greeting. They just looked at each other and then continued chatting as if I didn't exist. But the conversations seemed to be more furtive than before.

"...nearly killed Grace's husband..."

"...terrifying, the incompetence these days..."

"...have to keep an eye on her..."

My cheeks grew hot; even though I couldn't hear everything they were saying, I knew they were talking about me. I ducked my head and went into the shop.

The grocer's was better stocked than I'd anticipated; I supposed the railway had made it easier to bring in goods. A long wooden counter ran down the left-hand side of the store, behind which were shelves lined with tins of tea and biscuits, and jars of jam and preserves. Under the counter sat large hopper bins of sugar, flour and oatmeal. They even stocked luxuries like ladies' face powder, although the prices were exorbitant. The haberdashery section, with its bolts of fabric and cutting counter, was on the opposite side of the shop, while hardware was stored towards the back. There was even a small stand of fresh vegetables.

The white-aproned man behind the counter—Mr Smith, I presumed—looked me up and down unsmilingly, but said nothing as I went through my shopping list. I was mindful that I had to make the money last until my first pay, but I'd always been a good housekeeper, even if I hadn't been much of a wife, and I knew how to stretch a penny. As I waited, the store cat, which had been dozing on the countertop, stretched luxuriantly then wandered over and rubbed his face against my hand. It was the first token of affection I'd had for a long time.

Mr Smith wrapped up everything for me in brown paper and string and packed it neatly into my basket. The next stop was the butcher, for soup bones, and after that the blacksmith—for although I'd found a hatchet in the cottage for chopping wood, the shaft was so badly split that the head came off in my hand, and it was so blunt and rusty as to be all but useless anyway.

As I walked down the street it was as if a cloud was spreading out around me, quieting the happiness and bustle; people stopped and stared openly, seemingly not caring if I noticed them. I wondered if it was just because I was a stranger, and that was what people did in small towns, or if they'd already heard about what happened with the level crossing. I took a deep breath to steady myself, but I could feel their glances boring like needles between my shoulder blades.

There were one or two other people in the butcher's shop, but although they looked up when I entered, none of them spoke to me. I took my meat and left with barely a word exchanged. I couldn't imagine living like this every day for the rest of my life. The thought stirred a lump in my throat and an ache in my chest.

The blacksmith's shop was at the end of the main street. Inside there was the clang of a hammer as the smith re-shoed a horse. I paused in the doorway, watching, for smithery had always fascinated me. If I'd been born a lad, I thought I would have been a blacksmith. There was something visceral about taking a material as apparently unbreakable as iron and bending it to your will.

I just wanted to get my hatchet and go home, but there were other customers waiting ahead of me. I peered further into the dimly-lit smithy, feeling suddenly nervous, until I realised that one of them was Alec. Relief surged through me—at last, someone who'd be nice to me. He was talking to a man and a woman, both of whom had their backs to me. The woman's gown was a rich, dark purple, more sumptuous and expensive-looking than I'd have expected in a Tungold lady.

With a hiss and a spurt of steam, the smith quenched the new-made horseshoe in water, then looked up and saw me standing there.

"Can I help you, Miss?" Although I still wore a wedding band, people often mistook me for an unmarried girl, even in my 'half-mourning' attire.

"I need a hatchet, please."

"Just lemme finish this job and I'll be right with you."

"Of course." I could have watched him work all day.

Alec looked up at the smith's words and noticed me. His eyes crinkled in a smile and he waved me over.

"Mrs Adams," he said. "Good to see you."

"Likewise, Constable."

He turned to his companions. "Let me introduce you. Jane Adams, this is Peter Maloney and his wife Grace. Mr Maloney owns Queensgrace, the property down at the bottom of the escarpment. Mrs Adams is the new railway gatekeeper." The tone in his voice made it quite clear that Queensgrace was no small farm, and that Mr Maloney was a man of some influence.

Mr Maloney turned to me, and my heart sank as I recognised the man in the cart. Of all the people to nearly put under a train, I had to choose the local squatter.

"We've met," he said. His wife, a tall, strapping lady of around forty, with iron-grey hair and eyes to match, looked me up and down and was clearly displeased with what she saw. It was evident from the scorn in her glance that her husband had told her all about the incident.

"Anyhow, we must be going," Mr Maloney said, turning back to Alec. "I take it we'll see you at the dance tomorrow night?"

"Of course," Alec said affably, oblivious to the tension that was floating around us like thick fog. "Wouldn't miss it." I tried to ignore the conversation, because it was the first I'd heard of any dance, and if the day's reception had been any indication, an invitation was unlikely to be forthcoming.

"Although," Alec continued, "I'm in need of a partner. I don't suppose you'd do me the honour, Mrs Adams?"

To say I was shocked would not do the scene justice—but if anything, the Maloneys were even more so. Mrs Maloney looked like she'd bitten into a piece of rotten fruit, and while her husband covered his surprise better, it was clear he wasn't exactly thrilled by this new development.

For a moment I thought about refusing Alec's invitation, but then I steeled myself. I couldn't cower at home for the rest of my life, and this could be a good chance to start redeeming myself in the eyes of the town. I might even make some pleasant new acquaintances; surely Alec couldn't be the only friendly person in Tungold.

"Thank you, Constable. I'd love to come." I could see Mrs Maloney's lips twitching, but even with their relative power in the district, the squatter and his wife seemed reluctant to go against the policeman over something so trivial.

"Excuse me," Mrs Maloney said. "I believe I've just seen Edith Carter. I really must speak to her." She bustled out of the smithy and I watched her hurry across the street to the small gaggle of ladies I'd seen earlier at the grocer's. From the way they shot glances back towards the blacksmith's, I could tell they were talking about me.

"All done, Constable," the smith interjected, gesturing towards the horse. Alec paid him and took the reins. "Now, a hatchet, was it?" the smith asked, turning to me.

"Yes, please."

"It was good to see you again, Mrs Adams," Alec said as the blacksmith went to fetch the required article. "I'll call for you at six o'clock tomorrow evening."

"I look forward to it." I hoped I wasn't blushing. I stared after Alec as he led the horse away, thankful that there'd been at least one bright patch in the day.

"You want to watch yourself," Peter Maloney said softly. I turned to find him at my shoulder, far too close for propriety, and my heart began to race. He wasn't a tall man, but he was solidly built, and he still managed to convey a towering air of menace.

"What do you mean?"

"You need to be careful around the railway line. The ghost train comes for the unwary." He glared at me.

"I don't believe in ghosts."

"That's what Lily said too," he said with a shrug, letting the implication hang between us. "In this town it's safest to keep your head down and your nose out of other people's business, if you know what I mean."

My heart was pounding, but I'd never liked bullies. "Are you threatening me?"

He chuckled as if I'd made a joke, but the smile didn't reach his eyes. "Of course not, Mrs Adams," he said. "What a ridiculous notion. I'm simply giving you a friendly warning.

Anyone else in town would do the same; we care about each other here. I just wouldn't want you ending up like Lily is all."

"Thank you for your concern, sir." I wiped my sweaty palms discreetly on my skirt, then clenched my fists to stop my hands shaking. Thankfully, the smith returned at that moment, and the tension in the air burst like a pricked balloon. I quickly paid for my hatchet and left, scuttling out into the bright sunlight. But when I glanced back over my shoulder, Mr Maloney was still standing in the shadow of the blacksmith's doorway, watching me.

CHAPTER 5

Accepting Alec's invitation to the town dance had seemed like a good idea in principle, but by the following day I'd begun to question the wisdom of my decision. That night I'd have to parade myself in front of everyone like prize livestock, waiting upon their judgement. They should have just formalised it and made it an actual display, I thought rather bitterly—at least then everyone would be honest about why they were there. It was exactly this sort of treatment that had made me leave Goulburn, and I was sick of being the subject of people's gossip and their cheap entertainment. But I'd brought it on myself, so I had little right to complain.

It will be fine, I told myself; *I may even make some new friends*. Then I thought back to how the townspeople had treated me so far and wondered. Peter Maloney's warning had unsettled me more than I'd cared to admit, although I was still puzzled as to why he'd think I'd interfere in his business in the first place. But at least there was Alec. I couldn't lie; it would be nice to see him again.

I spent the day in the garden because I found the physical exercise pleasantly distracting, and there was an undeniable sense of achievement that came with overlaying order onto chaos and creating something beautiful. Much of my gardening so far had been uprooting and chopping away, but soon the new life would spring back and everything would be literally roses.

I was weeding a bed near the woodpile, lost in daydreams and enjoying the feeling of the warm sun on my back, when out of the corner of my eye I noticed something moving. I sprang back with a cry as a dark brown snake, four feet long if it was an inch, slithered out of the woodpile and headed straight for me. I didn't stop to think but turned and ran, not even pausing for breath until I was up the verandah steps and inside the house with the door firmly closed. I slumped into one of the kitchen chairs, shaking, trying to force the air back into my lungs. There weren't many things I was afraid of, but snakes were one of them. I still remembered watching my much-loved dog, Billy, writhing in agony after being bitten by a brown snake, until Pa took his gun and put the poor beast out of its misery. Snakes were a fact of life out here—and they helped keep the vermin down—but I doubted I'd ever get used to them.

It might have been cowardly of me, but after that I was reluctant to go back into the garden. In any case, Alec was calling for me at six, so I abandoned work for the day and began my toilette, heating water on the stove for a proper bath. I had only one evening dress, a lavender silk that set off my eyes and hair. Ma had bought it for me shortly after I married Jim. It was the first really pretty dress I'd owned, at least as a grown woman, for when Jim and I met I'd really only been putting my hair up for a year or so. I loved its short sleeves and low neckline, and the exquisite beading and lace trim. Whenever I wore it—to Railway Institute balls and such—heads would turn. It was vain to say so, but of course I noticed, and Jim looked proud to have me on his arm. Even after his death I couldn't bear to part with it, not because it reminded me of him, but because in that dress I was someone different from just poor old plain Jane Adams. In that dress, I was desirable.

It wasn't the easiest garment to put on without assistance, but eventually I managed. I also dressed my hair as best I could, adorning it with a sprig of sweetly scented jasmine from the garden. The effect, when I examined myself in the looking glass, was decidedly pleasing, although it felt strange to see myself in colour again. Even though I was no longer in full mourning, my everyday dresses were all rather drab shades of grey or brown. Nevertheless, I was sure I'd make a favourable impression on the good folk of Tungold. I wondered what Grace Maloney would be wearing.

Just as the clock struck six, there was a knock at the door, and I opened it to find Alec standing on the step. He was dressed in what I imagined was his best suit, spit-and-polished to within an inch of his life, and the result was very pleasing. The cut of the suit showed off his broad shoulders, although I mentally scolded myself for looking at him in such a way. I did not need another man in my life.

"May I escort you to the dance?" he asked rather formally, offering his arm. I looked past him and saw a trap parked outside the gate.

"Thank you, yes," I said, collecting my shawl and pulling the door behind me. He helped me into the trap like the gentleman he was, and I couldn't help smiling, because I'd almost forgotten what it felt like to be treated with such attentiveness. Despite my own better judgement, I wished the drive were longer.

"Have you had a pleasant day?" he asked as the trap lurched forward.

"Mostly," I said, telling him about the snake. I could feel my cheeks burning at my admission of such cowardice, but if he believed me foolish he didn't say so.

"I have a half-day holiday on Saturday," he said. "If you're agreeable, I could help you with the garden."

"I couldn't ask that; there must be so many better things you wish to do with your time."

"No, really, I insist."

"Well, thank you, that's very kind."

Ordinarily, the main street would be deserted at this time of day, with nothing open except the pub. But tonight the shopkeepers had strung lanterns along the fronts of their stores, giving the place a cheerful, festive look in the early evening light. They clearly took their town dances seriously in Tungold.

The church hall was an ordinary weatherboard building, not so different from the houses in its construction. There was already a procession of traps, buggies and horses parked outside; it seemed that not just the townsfolk, but the farm workers and squatters from all around the district were in attendance. Alec tied the horse to a hitching post outside the apothecary's and helped me down. It's wasn't far to walk to the hall, but he offered me his arm anyway. Such courtesy seemed to come very naturally to him. I wondered if, as with Jim, it would fall away once I got to know him better. If I'd learned anything over the years, it was that you could never trust a charming man.

We entered the hall into a bustle of noise and light. Half the town seemed to be there already, and the wave of sound assaulted my ears. I was acutely aware of how few faces in the throng I recognised, and I was suddenly thankful for Alec's arm.

"Would you like some punch?" he asked as we found ourselves a reasonably quiet corner.

"That would be wonderful, thank you."

As he fought his way through the crowd to the food table—the ladies of the town had evidently been hard at work—I took the opportunity to survey my surroundings. The hall was basically just a large room, with a small stage at one end where a band was tuning up: a fiddle, a fife and a drum. It reminded me of the Irish music Ma and Da's friends used to play, jammed into our small front room. Ma would start out all demure, but after a while she'd hitch up her skirts and start dancing in the middle of the rug, her feet flying. I never saw her look so happy as when she was dancing. It was as if the music stirred something in her blood, something from the old country.

Alec returned with a cup of punch and I accepted it gratefully. "Who are all these people?" I asked, taking a sip.

"Well now," he said, looking around the room, "a good number of the lads here are farmhands and drovers who work for Peter Maloney; I take it you've gathered he owns most of the land hereabouts." The farm lads were the usual sort, and there were quite a few of them; I'd already noticed that women were in the minority here, but then so it was in many of these outlying towns, I understood. The lads would have come from all over, drawn by the promise of work, while their sisters remained back in Goulburn or Sydney Town or whatever small hamlet they grew up in. It was probably part of the reason I'd caused such a stir, turning up as a single woman on my own, without a brother or father to accompany me, much less a husband.

Alec was still conducting an inventory of the room in his systematic police way. He pointed to a tall, strongly built man of about fifty, with peppercorn hair and a kindly but determined face. Studying him, I had the feeling that this was a man who knew what he wanted and how to get it. "That's John Anderson, mayor of Tungold. He's a sensible and honourable man and a passionate advocate of the railway extension, which often puts him at odds with Mr Maloney."

"I would have thought Mr Maloney would want to see the railway extended. It would help his business, surely."

Alec shrugged. "You'd think so, but he's argued vehemently against it ever since it was proposed. That's small-town politics for you." I liked that he talked to me as if we were equals; most men would think it beneath them to discuss politics with a woman.

"Over there are James Brown and David Carter," Alec continued, pointing out two men deep in conversation. "Magistrate and doctor. Their wives, Jessie and Edith, are part of Grace Maloney's coterie, as is Esme Johnson, the local schoolmarm." He indicated a pair of middle-aged ladies who were talking to a small, rather prissy-looking woman in a pale brown dress. "You don't want to get on their wrong side." He chuckled to himself.

"I'm afraid I don't understand the joke."

"My apologies—I was just remembering an incident the other week. Grace Maloney is the president of the Women's Temperance League, as she and her hangers-on like to remind Annie Graham by periodically picketing the pub. I've been called on to resolve such disputes on more than one occasion."

I laughed, imagining poor Alec stuck between Grace and Annie. "Does the League have many members?" I recalled the rows of patrons in the pub on my first night in Tungold, and couldn't help thinking that Grace Maloney must have her work cut out for her.

"Not at all, just half a dozen or so, all of them friends of Grace. Annie won't be going out of business any time soon. If they couldn't drink, the men in this town would have nothing to do."

At that moment I spotted the woman herself, by her husband's side, dressed in a deep purple extravaganza. Her frame seemed to have been pulled and shoved into the creation with brute force, and her hat was in danger of taking someone's eye out. She looked over and intercepted my glance, but didn't smile.

"And who's that?" I asked, my attention drawn away from Grace to a strange little man in what appeared to be a dress or robes of some kind.

"That's Charlie Chin," Alec said. "He doesn't normally get about in his Chinese ceremonial gear, but I guess tonight is a special occasion." He grinned. "He's a jack-of-all-trades, is Charlie. Runs a market garden now, but started out as a prospector on the goldfields. Apparently he's also a dab hand with explosives and fireworks and things of that sort. I hear there's going to be quite a show later."

"Really?" I'd only ever seen fireworks once before, when I was just a child. I remembered being both mesmerised and terrified. It had been a thrilling experience.

The band had finished tuning by now, and launched into a reel. I felt my toes begin to tap of their own accord; like Ma, music was in my blood.

"Dance with me?" I asked Alec impulsively. I knew it wasn't the done thing for ladies to ask, but I'd never really been one for rules. He looked a bit startled, then grinned.

"Come on then." He led me to the floor. Thankfully I knew the steps, although some of the locals did things slightly differently from what I was used to. But we made it through without any toes being trod on, and at the end of it I was flushed and laughing.

We danced three more dances, and I noticed surreptitiously that people were watching. There were some appreciative stares from the men—the dress was clearly doing its work—but I also saw Grace Maloney and Esme Johnson tittering together and shooting me looks that would curdle milk. I sighed, trying to ignore them, then changed my mind. I'd had enough of this.

"Good evening, ladies," I said, walking over to them as the dance ended. "What a lovely event this is."

"Thank you," Grace Maloney said, inclining her head regally. I wasn't aware I was paying her a personal compliment, but there it was.

"Grace organised it almost single-handedly," Esme chipped in, and I could see Grace Maloney swelling with pride in spite of herself.

"We may be a small town, but when we do things, we do them properly," she said. I'd have thought she was softening towards me except for the slight edge to her voice, as if she expected me to challenge her on the conduct of the evening. Unfortunately I'd never been one to walk away from a fight, but I'd learned in recent years that women did it very differently to men. I honestly thought it would have been easier if we could have just sorted things out with fisticuffs like the blokes did.

"It's been many years since I've been to a small country dance," I said. "It's charming, really charming." I let a hint of condescension creep into my voice, as if I'd come from Sydney Town rather than Goulburn. I knew I shouldn't antagonise this woman, but I couldn't seem to help myself. I just couldn't stand people who liked to crush others under their heels.

She glanced at someone over my shoulder. "Oh look, it's Jessie Brown," she said, as if she hadn't already spent half the evening talking to the magistrate's wife. "Do excuse me." She bustled off and Esme, muttering an excuse, followed. I shrugged and wandered over to the food table, reflecting that I clearly wasn't seeking an easy life.

Apart from Alec, very few people talked to me. The men were all somebody's sons or husbands, and although some of them shot appreciative glances my way, their wives and mothers were quick to prevent any closer contact. I noticed Grace speaking animatedly to her son after he made the mistake of saying hello to me. They buzzed with threat like a flock of sheep with a fox in their midst, these women, and I found it amusing until I overheard the word 'hussy' more than once. I tried to cover the ache in my chest with coquettish good-humour—which would surely rile the ladies even more—but I wasn't sure how well I succeeded.

My enjoyment of the evening was beginning to wane when Alec returned to my side. "Ready for the fireworks?" he asked. People had begun trickling out of the hall into the paddock behind it, where Charlie Chin was going to work his magic. I was about ready to go home, but I didn't let him see how miserable I was feeling.

The fireworks, however, did something to lift my spirits. They surged skywards, exploding in showers of red and gold sparks that rained down on the heads of the spellbound crowd. There was something magical about them, something not quite of this world. I wondered how Charlie Chin did it. It was one of those great mysteries of science to me, how a few chemicals mixed in exactly the right quantities could produce something so transporting.

I stood close to Alec in the throng, our shoulders touching slightly, which I couldn't deny was also something of a thrill. He looked rapt, like a child, face upturned in wonder at the spectacle.

As the last firework exploded and the field went dark, I heard sounds of a scuffle nearby, on the edge of the crowd. Somebody fetched a lantern, and in the flickering light I could see two men confronting each other in that way men do before things get ugly. One of the men was the mayor, John Anderson; the other was Peter Maloney. They were close enough that I could hear every acid-filled word.

"You've a nerve showing your face here," Mr Maloney said, his face just close enough to Mr Anderson's to be threatening. "You're going to be the ruin of us all, you and your ideas."

Mr Anderson scoffed, not backing down. If anything, he leaned closer, towering over the rather dumpy Mr Maloney. "The ruin? Hardly. Once the railway is extended, this town will prosper. You're a silly little man if you think otherwise."

"If the railway extension were to go through—and I will make sure it doesn't—all that would happen would be that our young men would leave town for work elsewhere."

"They can already leave town if they want to, and they are," the mayor replied, with what seemed to me to be impeccable logic. "The only ones remaining are the good-for-nothings like your Matthew who can't hold down a decent job!"

"Don't you slight my boy!" Peter yelled, launching himself at the taller man. "I'll kill you!" he shouted as he pummelled the mayor, losing all control. The crowd began to cheer at the prospect of a fistfight. Alec sighed and rolled his eyes.

"Excuse me," he said, nodding to me. "Duty calls." Then he walked over, calmly pushing his way through the throng that had gathered around the men, who were throwing rather ineffectual punches at each other. *Jim could've taught them a thing or two*, I thought, remembering how he used to bare-knuckle box for money or drinks. Mostly drinks.

"Gentlemen," Alec said, inserting himself into the fray. A couple of the other men helped him pull the two fighters off each other. "Gentlemen, really. There are women and children here. This is unbecoming to all concerned, and you are both leaders of the district. So unless you wish to settle this as cell-mates, I suggest you shake hands and go your separate ways." He was very calm as he said this, but there was steel in his voice and it was clear he meant what he said. The two men glared at each other but gradually seemed to realise the scrutiny they were under. John Anderson extended his hand and Peter Maloney reluctantly accepted it. "Good fellows," Alec said as they returned to their families and left the field. I understood now why he'd won the town's respect.

The evening wound down after that; nothing could really top a fight for entertainment value. Alec offered to drive me home and I accepted gratefully. My feet were sore from all the dancing, and there was still the mail train to see to.

"What was that all about?" I asked as we left the lights of the town behind us.

"Those two have had it in for each other for years, from what I can tell," he said. "Anderson wants development, and he's a big advocate of repairing and extending the old railway line. But Maloney for some reason has taken against it. I don't really understand why. But those who were here when the big accident happened all seem to be against extending the line again."

"They think it's haunted," I said.

"Really? I haven't heard that one."

"So no one's told you about the ghost train?"

He shook his head, grinning. "A ghost train? Whatever next?"

"A lot of them seem to think that Lily died because she saw the ghost train."

"However Lily Jacobs died, I doubt ghosts had much to do with it. In my experience, there's always a more prosaic explanation for these things."

We reached my gate, and he jumped down to help me out.

"Thank you for a lovely evening," I said.

"Likewise. It was most enjoyable, despite our esteemed leaders' best efforts." He smiled wryly.

"And if I ever see the ghost train I'll let you know—assuming I live to tell the tale, of course." I laughed.

"Please do," he said, returning my grin. "I like a good mystery. It makes a change from breaking up fistfights."

Inside, I relieved myself of my finery and changed back into an everyday gown. The mail train came through at ten, and afterwards I took myself gratefully to bed. Conflicting feelings about the night's proceedings swirled in my chest—the familiar, dull ache when I thought of the women's gossip, and a flutter of girlish nervousness when I recalled Alec's touch in the moonlight. At last I dozed off, to be captured by dreams of jewel-coloured dancers flitting like butterflies.

It was deep night when I was jerked from my slumber by the rattle of wheels. The full moon was streaming in through the window, and by its light I could read the clock on the mantelpiece: ten past four.

The sound was unmistakable: the clatter and clank of a train. Pulling on my slippers and wrapping a shawl around my shoulders, I hurried out onto the verandah. The night air was balmy, but even so, I shivered. I ran along the verandah to the side closest to the railway line, and there it was, before my very eyes: the ghost train.

It was a locomotive and a single wagon—not a carriage as Mr Bailey had described—moving quite slowly, puffing steam. Smoke gushed from the funnel. The locomotive was black, I thought, but it glowed with a strange, eerie luminescence, independent of the moonlight. The wagon, too, glowed with a weird light. Mr Bailey had said there was no driver, but as I peered towards the cabin I caught sight of someone. Then he turned toward me and I thrust my hands to my mouth to muffle a scream, for the driver was also shimmering, except for his eyes, which were just deep black holes in his head. I turned and ran back along the verandah, my shawl falling unheeded from my shoulders, and into the cottage, slamming the door behind me. When I reached my bedroom I dived into bed and pulled the covers up over my head, just as Mr Bailey had told me to do.

CHAPTER 6

When I woke the next morning it took me a few moments to remember why I felt uneasy. I lay there in a shaft of sunlight as it all came back to me: the rattle of the wheels, the eerie glow of the engine; the spectral driver. I shook my head, thinking it must have been an unusually vivid nightmare—unsurprising, with all the stories I'd been told. I rose and dressed, telling myself not to be silly.

It was only when I made myself a cup of tea and took it out to the verandah to drink in the sunshine that I saw it: my shawl, lying in a tangled heap where it had fallen during my headlong flight the previous night. I picked it up, running the soft wool between my thumb and fingers. So it wasn't a dream after all; I really had been out here in the dark, and I'd really seen the ghost train. That meant that all the stories I'd been told were true. Or did it? Perhaps it just meant that someone wanted me to think they were.

I shook my head, confused by my own thoughts. I needed someone sensible to discuss this with, someone logical who wasn't easily moved by flights of fancy. Someone like a policeman.

I finished my tea and readied myself to go out. Picking up my basket, I walked into town, as I'd been doing most days, but this time I wasn't on a shopping excursion. I ignored the people milling around the stores and went straight to the police station.

"Hello," Alec said in surprise, looking up from whatever paperwork he was doing. The police station was small but functional, with a front desk and waiting area, and a hallway that I assumed led to the station's small cells.

"What brings you here? Not coming to report a crime, I hope?"

"No...not exactly," I said, wondering now about the wisdom of this decision. Perhaps he'd just think me an hysterical woman and dismiss me entirely. It was certainly a strange enough tale. "I've seen the ghost train."

His eyebrows rose, but to his credit he didn't laugh at me. "Really? Can you describe it?" I told him everything I could remember, from the eerie glow to the ghostly driver, and he noted it all down dutifully.

"And you say it was noisy?"

"Yes—it rattled and crashed just like a normal train. I could see the steam and smoke as well."

"I would have thought a ghost train wouldn't need to be powered by actual coal," he said thoughtfully. "And surely it wouldn't rattle along the rails; it would just glide over them?"

I shrugged. "I suppose. I've never encountered a ghost—in locomotive form or otherwise—so I wouldn't know. What are you saying?"

"Are you sure it was really a ghost? Not just a train painted to look that way?"

"I don't know," I said, shaking my head, because by that point it was all becoming a bit of a muddle. "It's possible, I suppose. But I've never seen anything like that glow, and how do you explain the driver?"

"I'm not sure," Alec said. "But the whole thing is very strange, and smells more than a little fishy to me."

"Are you going to investigate it?"

"Perhaps. I'm intrigued. I told you, I like a good mystery. In the meantime, keep an eye out for it and let me know if you see it again."

"Of course. I could hardly miss it, I'm afraid. And you'll tell me if you discover anything about it?"

"You'll be the first to know."

I wandered back up the main street hardly aware of my surroundings, as my head was spinning so much from recent events. I felt reassured by Alec's reaction—at least he took me seriously—but I couldn't help wondering if I was going mad. I had no desire to see the terrifying ghost train again, and yet at the same time I wanted to prove to myself that I wasn't imagining it.

Annie Graham called out to me as I walked past the pub, startling me from my reverie and making me jump. She laughed.

"Hey there! You're a million miles away!"

"Yes, sorry." I was immediately suspicious of her friendliness; it was the first time anyone other than Alec had reached out to me, and she certainly hadn't seemed that well-disposed to me that first night in the pub. But maybe she was thawing.

"Everything all right?"

"Fine, thank you."

"I saw you going into the police station is all, so I was just wondering if something had happened." So that was it— she was after gossip. I wondered if I could trust her. She'd lived in Tungold a long time, so maybe she could shed some light on the whole ghost train story. And she was Grace Maloney's rival, which increased her standing ever so slightly in my estimation.

"Everything's fine, thanks. I just wanted to report something odd."

"Odd?"

"I saw the ghost train last night."

"*Did* you? What did it look like?"

I told her the same story I told Alec—the glow, the noise, the driver—and her eyebrows rose and rose until they were almost lost in her mop of curly red hair. Then, strangely, she dismissed me.

"I wouldn't worry about it," she said.

"It was pretty frightening. For a moment this morning I thought I'd dreamed it."

"Are you sure you didn't?"

"Yes, quite sure. Besides, I've heard other people have seen it too."

Annie sighed. "So they say, but the mind is a funny thing. When it hears the same story enough times it can start to tell you it's real."

"So you don't believe me? What about Lily?"

"Poor Lily was a bit touched in the head. It wasn't her fault; she was just born that way. She was a gentle soul, but she was inclined to have some strange ideas at times, and the ghost train was one of them."

"So how do you think she died?"

"I think she *thought* she saw the ghost train, no doubt about it," Annie said. "She wandered out onto the line late at night towards the end of winter and her constitution couldn't stand it. My guess is she died of exposure. Dr Carter said the same thing. Besides, people don't really die of fright, do they?"

I shrugged noncommittally. After what I'd seen last night—and I was sure I *did* see it—I was inclined to believe that anything was possible.

"If you want my advice," Annie said, "best you forget all about it. It's just a silly rumour that people like to spread round the town to scare new folk. I'm sorry that it's had this effect on you and I hope it won't happen again. It's quite disconcerting when our mind plays tricks on us like that."

"I don't think it was a trick," I said, but my heart wasn't really in it, and Annie just smiled indulgently.

"Never mind," she said. "Get a decent sleep tonight and I'm sure you'll feel better in the morning." She sounded like someone's kindly old mother, but there was a flicker in her eyes and I wondered if she was being entirely straight with me.

But our conversation was clearly finished, so I said my goodbyes and headed homewards.

I felt listless and out of sorts for the rest of the day; apart from Alec, I doubted anyone in town would believe me. They'd probably think I was delusional, if not an outright liar. I wondered if I'd ever fit in. But if I couldn't make it in this town of misfits, then I'd never make it anywhere. I didn't fit in in Goulburn right from the start, and there was no way I could go back there now. If Tungold rejected me too it would be a kind of death, for what point was there in living your whole life alone? I'd always envied the Grace Maloneys of the world, those who slotted so neatly into their communities and were looked up to and respected for their strength and competence. I'd never had the chance to lead anyone, and I wasn't sure anyone would ever want me to. I'd always been the one who lurked in the shadows, watching quietly from the edge of things. The social outcast, and now, it seemed, the crazy woman who invented ghosts out of harmless stories.

I'm ashamed to admit that I spent most of the afternoon in a rather self-indulgent fit of the mopes. I'd been resisting the homesickness for as long as I could—although quite what I was homesick for was hard to define, since I had no real home now but Tungold—but after my encounter with Annie it overcame me and I lay on my bed and wept. This went on for quite some time, until there were no tears left to shed. When it was over I felt exhausted and washed out, but also strangely relieved. Somehow, admitting to myself that not everything was perfect in this town, and that things were sometimes hard, made me feel better. I made myself a simple evening meal and went to bed early, resolving to try harder tomorrow. Thankfully, my sleep was unbroken by the noise of trains, ghostly or otherwise.

When I woke the next morning things seemed brighter, although the weather itself was a little dreary, with the sky overcast and grey, the precursor to a summer storm. I decided to walk into town again—because I needed to face my demons—and then be back in time to do my duty for the evening mail train. My days were falling into a pattern, and although I was grateful for the routine, and the income, I found myself craving excitement. But a walk into town was the best I could do for the time being.

I intended to call on Alec at the police station, although I knew he was unlikely to have discovered much in just a single day. But I just wanted to talk to someone who didn't think I was crazy. Unfortunately, however, I was thwarted in this aim outside the apothecary's, where I ran into Peter Maloney. I nodded politely to him and continued on my way, but he pulled me up.

"Mrs Adams, might I have a word?"

I sighed inwardly, but I had no choice. There were too many people watching for me to be outright rude to him. "Of course." I pasted my best smile on my face, although it pained me.

"I hear you've been asking questions about the ghost train."

There was hardly a sentence he could have uttered that would have taken me more by surprise. I didn't know what to say. I could only assume Alec had already begun making enquiries on my behalf, for how else would the squatter know? Unless Annie had told him.

"Well...I saw it the other night," I said, waiting for him to laugh. "But perhaps I just imagined it." It was easier if I deemed myself mad before he had the chance to. But he didn't laugh; in fact his eyes were cold and stony.

"Let me tell you, Mrs Adams," he said, lowering his voice, "the ghost train is real. And them that see it rarely live long afterwards, especially if they go blabbing or poking their noses in where they're not wanted."

I baulked at this, for it sounded suspiciously like a threat. "What are you saying?" I'd been threatened physically before, and being back on this familiar turf, however uncomfortable, somehow made me feel stronger. Perhaps I wasn't as mad as I'd thought.

"I'm just saying, watch yourself. Them spirits, they're not the kindly sort. This ain't no Christmas Carol, if you know what I mean." I thought of the ghosts in A Christmas Carol and almost laughed at the comparison, wondering if Mr Maloney had actually read it. He didn't seem to me to be a man of letters. I might not have had a great deal of formal schooling, but I'd managed to educate myself nonetheless. Da had insisted on it, and had spent what little spare money he had on books.

"Thank you, Mr Maloney. I shall bear your warning in mind." I spoke rather haughtily, for I didn't take kindly to people ordering me around, especially in such a blunt, heavy-handed way. Peter Maloney clearly lacked subtlety. And I wondered, why bother, really? What was he hiding? The previous day, Annie had all but convinced me that I'd imagined the ghost train and that the whole thing was best forgotten. Now I wasn't so sure, for if it was important enough for the squatter to personally warn me off then perhaps there was more to the story than I'd first thought.

"You do that," he said, getting close enough to make me uncomfortable. Despite myself, I jerked away. He gave me one final glare then turned on his heel and departed, leaving me trembling in his wake—with rage or fear, I couldn't quite tell.

I didn't see Alec again until Saturday, when he kept his promise to help me with the garden. As I helped him unload his tools, I was startled by the sound of clucking coming from a crate.

"What on earth is that?"

He grinned. "I thought you could use some company. Or at least some fresh eggs." He lifted the crate down and prised the lid off. Inside were two brown hens, clucking and pecking at each other in agitation. "They're good for the garden, and I'll build you a coop to put them in at night."

I didn't know what to say to this kindness. "I...thank you," I stammered eventually. "You didn't have to do that."

"I know," he said. "But I wanted to."

I named the hens Bertha and Estella and we turned them loose in the garden. They particularly loved the freshly dug areas, scratching around in the overturned earth for worms and insects. True to his word, Alec set about building them a coop from the various scraps of timber he found lying around the unkempt yard, while I continued cutting back the overgrown bushes, and weeding. It was such a pleasant afternoon that at one point I actually pinched myself to check I wasn't dreaming.

By the time the day was beginning to wane, the garden was looking much more respectable, and Bertha and Estella had a happy house in which to roost. I saw Alec off with a smile and a wave, promising him fresh eggs whenever I could spare them.

As I washed myself and prepared dinner, I pondered the events of the last week. The ghost train hadn't reappeared, but ever since my encounter with Peter Maloney I'd been unable to let the subject rest. I hadn't heeded his warning, if that was what it was, and I'd continued asking discreet questions where possible, but no one had been able to enlighten me. I wondered who else I could ask.

I pondered this for a while, and then the answer came to me. There was someone who might know, but I really, really didn't want to ask him. I decided to sleep on it.

The next morning I revisited the idea. It was still as unpalatable to me as it had been the previous night, but I didn't see that there was much other choice. I decided to walk into town anyway; I could always withdraw right up until the moment I was standing in front of him.

I released Bertha and Estella to roam around the garden, then made for town. There was a mugginess in the air that was oppressive; it felt harder to breathe, somehow, and even though my dress was light, I was perspiring heavily before I was halfway there.

It wasn't until I entered the deserted main street that I remembered that of course it was Sunday. Even the pub was closed, and everyone was either in church or lying low. It had been a long time since I'd darkened the door of a church—not since my wedding, in fact—and I wasn't about to start now, although I had ample choice; despite its small size, Tungold was home to three congregations. I was just berating myself for my own stupidity in not considering the time—for now I'd had a wasted journey and would have to come back in the afternoon—when St Paul's threw open its doors, spilling worshippers into the street. I peered through the cluster of people, looking for the one I was seeking, and then I saw him—jowly and bullish, talking to Alec, of all people, and scribbling something on a little notepad in his hand. I took a deep breath and made my way through the throng, until I was so close they couldn't help but notice me.

"Jane," Alec said, his face lighting up. "How lovely to see you." He turned to his companion.

"Mr Brian Mathieson, let me introduce Mrs Jane Adams. Mrs Adams is our new level crossing gatekeeper. Mr Mathieson is from the Railway Board and is here to investigate the reopening of the old line."

"Mr Mathieson," I said. "Pleased to meet you."

He finished whatever he was writing and tore off the sheet. "Likewise, Mrs Adams." For some reason we'd clearly decided to pretend that we didn't know each other.

"George Bailey mentioned you'd recently arrived," he added. "I'm sorry for your loss. Such a terrible thing to lose your husband in an *accident* like that."

"Thank you." I narrowed my eyes, wondering what he was playing at, but he said nothing further.

This deception made for a strange interaction. Brian and I steadfastly avoided addressing each other, while Alec chattered on, apparently oblivious.

"So, how are your enquiries going?" Alec asked. "I've heard you've met with a fair bit of opposition from the expected quarters."

Brian shrugged. "It's just a scoping study at this stage. I intend to examine the accident site and assess the condition of the line and how easy it will be to repair."

"I've heard it's in pretty poor shape," Alec said. "I haven't seen it myself, but they say it's overgrown and the rails are all buckled. Will you be looking at repairing it or redirecting the line entirely? The last thing the town needs is another accident."

"Of course," Brian said. "But my understanding is the accident was caused by human error. Besides, the cutting has already been made down the escarpment; even with the necessary repairs to the line, it would be far more expensive to have to redo that work elsewhere."

"It sounds like the plans are well-advanced."

"It's by no means decided," Brian said. "This is merely an exploratory survey. But I'm surprised to find such opposition to work that will surely be beneficial to the town. The construction will bring much-needed jobs to the area."

"That it will. But I'm sure you're no stranger to small-town politics."

"Indeed."

Throughout this exchange my stomach had been clenching with nerves, and I wondered how on earth I was going to bring up the subject of the ghost train. I waited for Alec to make his excuses and move on, giving me an opportunity, but when the conversation began to draw to a close he turned to me and asked if he could walk me home. Out of the corner of my eye, behind Alec's back, I could see Brian smirking.

"Of course," I said, even though it removed any chance I may have had of talking to Brian alone. I'd lost my nerve, for now at least, and anything that removed me from the situation was welcome. As I was leaving, he shook my hand.

"It was lovely to see you, Mrs Adams," he said with no trace of irony. "I hope we'll meet again soon."

"It's a small town, Mr Mathieson," I replied. "I'm sure we will." *Whether I liked it or not*, I mused. He held my hand just a fraction too long, and I didn't like what I saw in his eyes.

"Brian Mathieson seems a nice enough fellow," Alec said as we meandered down the road. The sun was blazing, but there were dark thunderheads forming away to the west.

"Yes, I suppose so," I said, causing him to glance at me strangely.

"You don't agree?"

"I hardly know the man. But he does seem very single-minded."

"That may not be a bad thing; it could be just what the town needs. All the young lads are leaving; there's just not enough work around here. If something doesn't change soon, the town will eventually disappear."

"Mr Maloney seems to think otherwise, from what I saw at the dance."

"I don't know whose interests Peter has at heart, but I'm not entirely sure they're Tungold's."

"So you think they should extend the railway line?"

"Why not? It's bound to happen eventually, so why not get the best deal for the town that they can?"

I shrugged. "I know nothing of business dealings."

"Then you should learn, especially since you're on your own. I don't believe this nonsense about women leaving money and politics to their husbands."

"Next thing you'll be saying women should have the vote!" I laughed, because I'd never heard a man talk this way before.

"I think they should. Don't you?"

"Of course, but there's precious little I can do about it."

"You have more power than you think. You have to take control of your own life; you're the only one who can change your situation."

"You think I don't know that?" I felt resentment creeping over me, for I knew better than anyone what it took to swing circumstances that weren't in one's favour. I'd done it, but it had cost me, and now here I was in this one-horse town, trying to start a new life.

Alec must have heard the edge in my voice, for he backed down. "Forgive me, I meant no offence."

"None taken." I smiled. He meant well, but I couldn't help feeling that Constable Ward's actions were blunted by his idealism.

We were just walking past the pub when there was a shout behind us. "Constable!" We turned around to find an elderly woman whom I didn't recognise, hobbling towards us as fast as she could. She was wearing widow's weeds and a distressed expression.

"Constable," she puffed, "I need your help! It's Bruce—he's stuck under the house!"

"Of course, Mrs Blake," Alec said. "I'll come right away. Sorry," he added, shooting me an apologetic look. "Duty calls."

"Who's Bruce?" I asked as Mrs Blake, not waiting for Alec, began shuffling back down the road. "Her son?" I was trying to picture all the circumstances in which a grown man could get himself stuck under a house, and what exactly Alec was going to do about it.

Alec laughed. "No," he said, "her cat. The blasted animal has a knack for getting itself wedged in the most ridiculous places. I'd better go. I'll see you soon?"

"I hope so. Good luck with the cat."

I walked home alone, pondering the strange conversation with Brian. Why did he refuse to acknowledge our acquaintance? I was lost in thought as I mechanically opened the garden gate and made my way up the now-cleared path, but I was brought back to myself by a strange buzzing noise. Climbing the verandah steps, I looked up and retched violently as my glance fell on the front door. Poor Bertha was nailed to the door at eye level, her throat slit, flies swarming around the fresh wound. On the adjoining wall was a message scrawled in rapidly darkening blood: *You'll be next*. And below it, like a signature, was the crude but unmistakable picture of a train.

CHAPTER 7

After I'd wiped the wall clean and cut poor Bertha down, I plucked her and made her into a pie, then boiled her bones for stock. She wasn't long dead, and I wasn't so well-off that I could afford to turn my nose up at fresh meat when it landed on my doorstep.

The work helped ease the shaking in my hands, although I made sure the doors and windows were locked, even though the day was stiflingly hot. The storm rolled in around mid-afternoon, and I stood at the kitchen window watching the light change. The sky was the colour of bruised flesh, the burnt browns and yellows of the garden standing out against it with unnatural vividness. Thunder rumbled in the distance, and every now and then a fork of lightning crackled across the horizon, but there was no rain. Carried on the wind was the unmistakable tang of smoke.

The initial rush of terror at finding Bertha's carcass and the terrible message had begun to dissipate, although I thought it would be sometime before I felt safe opening up the doors again. And the more I considered this, the angrier I became. Someone was clearly trying to warn me off the ghost train—they must have thought I was getting uncomfortably close to their secret, although in reality I knew very little beyond superstition and speculation. And not so long ago, such a warning would have worked. But I'd been through a lot in the last year or so, and I was no longer so easily cowed. If they were hoping I'd disappear, they'd be sadly mistaken. I gritted my teeth as I rolled out the pastry and draped it over the pie dish. There was nothing for it—I'd have to confront Brian Mathieson and find out what he knew.

The storm had blown itself out by the next morning, and the day was mercifully cooler. I was walking into town when I heard a horse and cart approaching behind me. I moved to the side of the road as it slowed and finally stopped. It was driven by Matthew Maloney, Peter and Grace's ginger-haired son.

"Can I offer you a lift, Mrs Adams?" he asked. I was a little taken aback, for this was the first time I'd had anything to do with the Maloney boy, and I'd expected him to be as snide as his parents, not a polite young man. But I had a blister starting on my heel, so I gratefully accepted.

"What brings you into town?" I asked as we trotted along.

"Just picking up some things for my dad," he said. He was taciturn without being rude; I had the feeling he was a bit shy. With such loud, opinionated parents, I supposed it was understandable, so I let the silence hang for a few minutes.

"Do you have any brothers and sisters?" I asked on impulse after it had dragged on long enough. It occurred to me that I knew very little about the Maloney clan.

"Nah, just me. You?"

"I'm the oldest of six. One sister and four brothers." Lottie was the only one I was still in contact with, but I didn't tell him that. It would require too much explanation.

"Golly."

We lapsed into silence again—I had the feeling he preferred it that way—and I watched the countryside roll by, drifting into a half-dream. It wasn't until we reached the outskirts of town, just near the pub, that I was snapped out of it.

There was a crowd of people milling in the road around the front of the hotel; they seemed to be looking at something. It was still quite early and I was at a loss as to what could possibly be drawing their attention. Matthew stopped the cart, for he couldn't get past, and I hopped down.

"What's going on?" I asked the first person I saw—a man I didn't know. He just shrugged and turned away. I spotted Annie Graham in the crowd and elbowed my way over to her, where I repeated my question. She looked exhausted and harried, her eyes red-rimmed and watery.

"Mrs Graham?"

"Oh, it's terrible," she said, gulping as if she was fighting back tears. "That poor man. I know he wasn't the easiest fellow to get along with, but really, no one deserves this."

"Who are you talking about? What's happened?" She just waved at the crowd and I peered through the throng of people to glimpse what they were all staring at: a long mound in the road, covered by a white sheet.

"Is that...?"

"Brian Mathieson—yes. The poor bloke fell off the balcony late last night. I didn't hear a thing and nobody realised until first thing this morning when Polly came to work and discovered him." I looked over to the verandah, where the maid was sitting in Annie's rocking chair, knees drawn up, visibly shaking. Esme Johnson was comforting her.

"That's awful!"

"I've never had anything like this happen here before. I just don't understand..."

"Perhaps he was drunk and he fell. The railings aren't that high."

"No, he wasn't," Alec said, coming over from where he'd been examining the body. "It's pretty clear there was a struggle. I think he was pushed."

"*Pushed?*" Annie gasped. "No, surely not! I mean, who would do such a thing?"

"That's what I intend to find out," Alec said grimly. "Mrs Graham, I'll need to speak to you and Polly properly once you're both feeling better."

"Shall I get you a glass of brandy?" I asked, and Annie nodded.

"In the kitchen pantry," she said. "I keep a bottle there for medicinal use."

I went into the pub and made my way to the large kitchen at the back. I found the pantry easily enough and fetched the bottle of brandy down from the shelf, along with two glasses, for I fancied Polly probably needed one too.

When I got back outside Alec was moving the crowd on, and Matthew Maloney was helping Dr Carter lift the body, still covered by its white sheet, into the bed of the cart. I wondered what they were going to do with it; I supposed if it was murder some sort of examination would be in order. The crowd dispersed slowly, little pockets of people dribbling down the road towards the shops, still talking animatedly. It was without a doubt the most exciting thing to happen in Tungold in quite some time, and as appalling as it was, I could understand the thrill they were probably feeling. In any case, from the shreds of conversation I'd overheard, Brian didn't seem to be well-liked in town, and there was less obvious grief than there would have been if it were a town stalwart who had been murdered.

After the body was removed, a large red stain still remained in the dirt of the road, reminding all who saw it of what had occurred. It turned my stomach slightly, and I looked away.

"How do you know he was murdered?" I asked Alec, catching him as he passed. "How do you know he didn't kill himself?"

"I don't think I should be telling you the gory details. It's really not appropriate."

"I can cope, I promise."

"Well, he had knife wounds on his hands. He wouldn't have done that to himself. If it was suicide, it was because someone forced him into it. They may not have actually pushed him, but they certainly put him in a position where the outcome was inevitable."

"That's horrible! Why would someone do such a thing?"

"Well, that's what I have to find out."

"I can help."

He stared at me, clearly taken aback. "What do you mean?"

"There's only one of you—you can't do it all on your own. I can take notes and things." It sounded weak, even to my ears, but the truth was I was bored and lonely. A little excitement was exactly what I needed.

"I don't think so."

"Please...just think about it."

He shot me another strange look, his brow furrowed, then walked away, shaking his head. I wondered what that meant.

Naturally, the murder was all anyone could talk about all day. Grace Maloney and her coterie were in their usual spot near the grocer's, and they were thriving on the gossip. I hadn't seen Grace look so radiant and energised since I arrived.

"Mrs Adams!" she called as she saw me passing. "Have you heard the news about Mr Mathieson?" Her burning desire to share the story near and far had apparently overridden the disdain she felt for me, at least temporarily.

"Why, yes," I said. "Awful, isn't it?"

"Who would have thought such a thing could happen in Tungold!" Edith Carter, the doctor's wife, piped up. When I was talking to this group I couldn't help feeling like I was in a play of some sort, the way each delivered her lines.

"Indeed," I said. "Any idea of who did it?"

"I can't possibly imagine," Grace said. "Tungold people are so kind and generous to each other. I've barely heard an angry word spoken, let alone witnessed something like this. It's unbelievable." I was amazed at the woman's ability to separate her ideas from any evidence to the contrary, given that it was only a short while ago that her own husband had come to very public blows with the local mayor, but I said nothing.

"Still," murmured Jessie Brown, the magistrate's wife, so meek and mild that I strained to hear her, "he was an *outsider*."

"Yes, quite," the others agreed. They seemed to have forgotten who they were talking to, or maybe they just didn't care.

"Do you think it was a local who killed him?" I asked. "Tungold doesn't seem to get a lot of strangers."

"No, surely not," Edith said. "I mean, we get those men who come to help with the mustering on the estate. It could have been anyone."

"He did rub a few people up the wrong way, though," Esme Johnson blurted out, having so far been silent.

"Really?" I asked, intrigued. It seemed I wasn't the only one Brian had got on the wrong side of. "Such as whom?"

"Well...I know Annie never really took to him. I mean, she's always polite—in her job she has to be—but I saw them having a very intense conversation the night before last, and she didn't look happy."

"What do you mean?"

"Well...she almost seemed to be...pleading."

"Surely not!" I couldn't imagine tough Annie Graham begging over anything.

"No, really. And he was just standing there, dismissive, nose in the air, as if he was taking the moral high ground on something."

"That's interesting." I wondered if I should tell Alec. It would probably come out when he interviewed Annie later anyway. "You said a few people," I reminded Esme. "Who else?"

She chewed her lip for a moment and glanced at Grace. "I don't know for sure," she said, "but I'm sure there were others. He just seemed to be disagreeable to everyone." I wondered if she was speaking from experience.

"He was an odious man," Grace said with some vehemence. "Rude, uncultured and buffoonish. I would never go so far as to wish harm on a person, but I doubt he'll be missed."

I narrowed my eyes at her, wondering whether to probe further. I wondered what Brian had done to warrant such a vicious assassination of his character. But there was a firm line to Grace's mouth and a hardness to her eyes that stopped me from pushing the issue.

I stayed a little longer with the ladies, but they seemed to have exhausted all their sources of useful information, and the discussion rapidly turned into idle speculation and a going-over of the facts. For supposedly cultured ladies, they seemed to have a morbid fascination with the mechanics of the death.

How exactly would a body have fallen from the balcony? Would he still have been alive after he hit the ground? How high did a fall have to be to kill someone instantly? On and on it went, until I was feeling slightly sick to my stomach. I made my excuses and departed, wondering whether I should go home, or stay in town and try to find out more useful information. Perhaps I should tell Alec what I knew.

In the end, that was what I decided to do. He was sitting at his desk when I arrived at the police station, going through papers.

"Solved it yet?" I asked as I entered, trying to lighten the air of seriousness that hung over the room like a cloud. He looked up, recognised me and smiled. "Not yet," he said. "There's some interesting things coming to light, though."

"Really? Do tell."

"I can't, Jane. Police protocol and all that."

"Funny, you never struck me as a man who cared overly much about protocol." This, at least, was true.

"I still have to interview anyone who had anything to do with Brian while he was here, though," he said. "That includes you, you know."

"Really?"

"When I introduced you yesterday I got the feeling you may have already been acquainted."

My stomach lurched. Clearly our pretence hadn't been that convincing. I might have to tell the truth. I groaned inwardly, but there was nothing for it.

"Why don't you interview me now, then, since we're both here?"

He sighed, chewing it over. It seemed like he was starting to realise the size of the task before him. "Very well. Take a seat." I pulled up a chair on the other side of the desk from him and waited, apprehension fluttering faintly in my chest.

"How did you know Brian Mathieson?"

"He was my husband Jim's boss on the railway in Goulburn."

"Did you know him well?"

"Not at all—I only met him a couple of times. But I never really liked him."

"Why was that?"

"He was a bully. He liked to push people around in whatever way he could. From what I'm hearing in town, I'm not the only one with that impression. Nobody I know who met him liked him much, either here or in Goulburn."

"Did you have much to do with him after he came to Tungold?"

"No, not really. Yesterday was the only time I talked to him. As I said, I didn't like him and I didn't really want to socialise with him."

"Do you know who may have wanted to kill him?"

I shook my head. "It could have been anyone. Like I said, I understand he wasn't well liked in town."

"Doctor Carter is doing an examination as we speak, but we found this on the desk in the hotel room," Alec said, pushing a piece of paper across the table to me. There was something scrawled on it in pencil, the words circled for emphasis.

"*J.A. murder*," I read, surprised. "What does that mean?"

Alec shakes his head. "I don't know. Any ideas?"

I thought for a moment, chewing my lip. "It couldn't have anything to do with John Anderson, could it? The mayor?"

"What do you mean?"

"Well, there's been all this controversy over the railway extension. John Anderson really wants it to happen, but some in the town are firmly against it. And Brian Mathieson was here to do a study on the feasibility of the extension. What if he found out that someone was planning to murder John Anderson to stop the extension taking place? And then that same person realised that he knew about the plot, and had to silence him?"

Alec looked stunned at this, but then he shrugged. "The issue of the railway has certainly been inflaming passions around here lately."

"Yes," I said enthusiastically, glad that he was giving my idea credence. "I mean, remember the dance, where Peter Maloney and John Anderson got into that fight? You don't think Peter could have had something to do with it? Or what about the ghost train? Is it possible the two things could be connected?"

He shrugged again, shaking his head. "I don't know. It's really too early to say at this point. Is there anything else you'd like to tell me?"

I paused, thinking about poor Bertha and the warning on my wall. "No."

CHAPTER 8

T he next morning, as soon as decorum allowed, I walked into town to call on Alec. I half-expected the police station to be buzzing with activity, for surely a murder warranted a little fuss. I assumed Alec would have reported it to the other police in the district and to his superiors in Goulburn. It would probably take at least a day for someone to arrive from Goulburn, but an officer could doubtless be spared from one of the local stations in the neighbouring towns. But there was no one there except Alec.

"Good morning," he said, looking up as I entered.

"Morning. Where is everyone?"

"What do you mean?"

I explained what I'd been expecting, about the other police coming in from Goulburn and the surrounding areas. "I wouldn't have thought they see that many murders. In my experience, people always want in on the action at times like this."

He flushed, and I wondered what he wasn't telling me. Then something clicked.

"You haven't notified them, have you?" I was a bit amazed by this—a young country constable withholding information from his superiors about a serious crime in his district?

"No."

"Why on earth not?"

"It's complicated."

"The most interesting stories usually are. What's going on?" I removed my hat and gloves and took a seat at the desk without waiting for an invitation, making myself at home.

"Do you remember how you asked why I came to Tungold, and I told you I didn't have a choice?"

I nodded. "Of course."

"It wasn't an ordinary posting. I used to be based at Berrima. We got a lot of action up near Bargo, mainly chasing bushrangers and other thugs out of the Bargo Brush. You know it?"

"I know of it. But I thought it was much better now." Da had told me stories of the infamous Bargo Brush. It was an area on the road between Goulburn and Sydney at the bottom of the range known as the Razorback. In the days before the railway came, the coaches had been forced to travel that way, and often got bogged or stranded in the mire. The bush was thick and almost impenetrable, making it the perfect haven for bushrangers, who would accost the stricken coaches, robbing travellers and stealing money and others goods from the mailbags. The bushrangers' reign had declined with the coming of the railway, but there were still enough vagrants around that the pastoralists all locked their doors and kept a close watch over their livestock.

"It is. But this was a while ago, and some of the ruffians are still out there. Anyhow, my team and I got into a shoot-out with a gang. You've heard of Captain Starlight?"

I nodded. Captain Starlight was the most infamous bushranger of them all. He'd started out as a cattle rustler but had graduated to robbery and more nefarious things. I'd never been quite sure whether to be scared or awed at his exploits.

"Long story short, I was shot in the leg. One of the other fellows got me out of there, and we captured a couple of the gang members, but Starlight got away. Anyhow, my leg was in a bad way. For a bit there it was uncertain if they'd be able to save it. It came good eventually, but I was sent back to Berrima and put on light duties. Even after I could walk and ride again, I still had a limp, and the sergeant wouldn't let me go back to what I'd been doing. Said it was too dangerous, even though I would have been almost ready for promotion if the incident hadn't happened. Then Constable Jenkins retired and they decided to send me here." He sounded bitter and angry—two things I never would have expected from cheerful, charming Constable Ward. But to have such a promising career snatched away like that would, I supposed, make anyone bitter. I thought I understood now why he hadn't reported Brian Mathieson's murder.

"So you want to prove yourself to them by solving this?" I said. "Show them that you're worthy of more than just being stuck breaking up bar fights in a one-horse town?"

"It sounds ridiculous when you put it like that, doesn't it?" he said. "But yes, I suppose that's the nub of it."

"I understand what it's like to have to prove yourself," I said. I understood perhaps better than he knew, for I felt like I'd spent my whole life having to prove myself to someone or other—that I was a good daughter, a good wife, and now a good employee and citizen of Tungold. When you've never found your place, you spend a lot of time trying to prove to others—and to yourself—that you fit, that you're somehow deserving of the belonging they take for granted.

"Funny, I wouldn't have thought that," he said. "You seem like a natural leader to me."

I laughed at this. "I've never led anyone in my life. I'm just a railway girl—what would I know about that?"

He shrugged. "Sometimes we surprise ourselves. You're probably capable of more than you think."

"Perhaps."

We sat in silence for a few minutes, Alec filling out papers while I stared out the window.

"Have you thought any more about my theory?" I asked eventually.

"Which one?"

"About Peter Maloney and the railway. Surely it fits too neatly to be anything else—they must be connected."

"Coincidences are more common than you'd imagine."

"So you're not going to investigate it?"

"I didn't say that. I'm going to be following all leads. And yes, I acknowledge that the railway does seem to be at the centre of things." He looked at me for a long moment then relented. "Actually, I'm about to head out to Queensgrace to talk to Mr Maloney now. Would you like to come?"

"Really?"

"As my scribe."

"I'd love to."

He stood up, then paused. "Just before we start," he said, "we need to get a few things straight. I appreciate your offer to scribe, and I'm keen to take you up on it, because you're right that I can't do it on my own. But this is my investigation and everything needs to be done according to police procedure. In the interview you just take notes; you don't ask questions and you don't put forward theories. Is that clear?"

"Crystal." If I hadn't put forward my theory about John Anderson and Peter Maloney we'd have nothing to go on at all, but I decided not to point that out to him. Some rules were made to be broken.

"Have you been out to Queensgrace before?"

"No. What's Queensgrace?"

"It's the name of the Maloney property."

"Oh." How...*regal*.

There was a small pony trap housed in the yard behind the police station, and a grey mare in the paddock opposite. I guessed Alec would normally ride if he had to go places, but with me tagging along the trap was the better option. He caught the horse expertly and harnessed her with ease, then helped me up.

We drove back through town, past my cottage and over the railway line, then took a pleasant country road that ran parallel to the line for a while. After a bit the road began to wind down a steep escarpment and Alec slowed the horse to a walk to better negotiate the switchback turns. The railway line had veered away and was no longer visible through the trees, but I imagined the site of the old accident must be somewhere around there. I mentioned it to Alec.

"Yes, I think so," he said. "I haven't seen it myself, but I believe the train lost its brakes as it was going down the hill, so it must be close by."

As we reached the bottom of the escarpment, the country opened up before us into wide, fertile paddocks, burned brown by the sun. It was clearly good country and I could see now how men like Peter Maloney had made their fortunes farming it. But I failed to see why he was so opposed to the railway extension—having to bring carts of produce up the escarpment, even though it wasn't actually all that far to Tungold, must have been trying for his business. Being able to load it all onto a train right outside his farm would make so much more sense.

The entrance to Queensgrace was marked by a neat wooden fence and a set of wrought iron gates, fancy for a country property. The driveway was long and winding, and Alec told me that pretty much all the land thereabouts belonged to the Maloney family. We saw fields of crops, as well as sheep grazing. As we approached the homestead we drove through a beautifully cultivated garden, clearly someone's pride and joy. I wondered if Grace had a softer side.

A maid answered our knock and led us into a pleasant parlour. The house smelled of furniture polish and was scrupulously clean. The furniture, likewise, was of a better quality than I was used to seeing, and there were sumptuous rugs on the floor. The Maloneys were clearly doing quite well for themselves.

We were left to sit longer than was strictly polite, and I wondered if Peter was trying to remind us of where the power lay. But eventually he entered, although he made no apology for keeping us waiting.

"Constable," he said, nodding to Alec. "And Mrs Adams, I see. What's your role in all this?"

Alec explained about my scribing duties, and Peter nodded, although he still looked sceptical. "Well, I don't really have much to say, Constable," he said, "so I'm afraid you're wasting your time."

"Tell me about the railway."

"What about it?"

"You're opposed to the extension, correct?"

"I think that's common knowledge."

"Why is that?"

Peter Maloney looked a bit affronted at having to explain himself—it was as if everyone had always just taken the reasons for his opposition for granted and had never really bothered to ask about them.

"Well," he blustered, "it'll be bad for the town. It won't bring the jobs like they say it will, and it'll destroy our way of life. And then there's the risks. You've been here all of ten minutes, young man, so you don't remember the accident. But I was born and grew up here, and I remember it well. We can't have another tragedy like that on our hands, which is what'll happen if the line gets extended."

I stared at him, slightly surprised that his reasons were so flimsy. It seemed to me that, even taking all this into account, the benefits of the railway for his business still far outweighed the potential pitfalls. And Peter seemed cagey, wary even. I remembered his warning about the ghost train, and wondered if jobs and safety were the only reasons he opposed the line extension.

"So I take it you didn't like Brian Mathieson very much, then," Alec said.

Peter shrugged. "Just another bloody bureaucrat, from what I could tell," he said.

"Please watch your language, sir," Alec said. "There's a lady present." I nearly laughed out loud at this, thinking of the screaming rows Jim and I used to have, which would have made Alec's ears burn if he could have heard them. I may have been many things, but not many people had accused me of being a lady.

"Apologies, Mrs Adams," Peter said. "It's just that we've seen a lot of them down this way over the years, and they're all the same. Sticking their noses in where they're not wanted."

"Did Brian get involved in something he shouldn't have?" Alec asked.

"How would I know? It's got nothing to do with me."

"He wanted to go and see the accident site, is that right?"

"What of it?"

"Did you take him there?"

"No. I went to see him to arrange a time to go, but of course then someone knocked him off."

"So you went to see him the night he died?"

"Yes. Straight after dinner. The bloody lout called me all sorts of names. But I didn't kill him, if that's what you're asking. It was a short meeting and I came straight home afterwards. Ask any of the servants—they saw me."

"And your wife?"

91

"She wasn't here. Probably at some Ladies' Auxiliary meeting or something."

"So you saw him at what, around seven o'clock, and then you went straight home?"

"I just said that, didn't I? I think it's time you went and bothered someone else. We're finished here." He stood up abruptly and it was clear we were dismissed. If we wanted answers, we'd have to look elsewhere.

CHAPTER 9

"Something wasn't right about that," I said as we drove back to Tungold. "There's something he's not telling us."

"You think so?"

"Of course—wasn't it obvious?"

"I suppose."

I stared at Alec, amazed that he couldn't tell that Peter had been lying—it had been written all over the squatter's face. I wondered if Alec's injury was the only reason he'd been sent to Tungold, or if his superiors had also had concerns about his performance. He was a nice man, but a tad gormless. If I'd wanted to, I could have walked all over him. I wondered if he was shrewd enough to take on the likes of Peter Maloney.

"So who are we talking to next?" I asked.

He shook his head. "No one yet. I want to go back to the station and write up these notes to try to get some things clear in my mind. It seems like half the town had it in for Brian Mathieson, and we'll have to talk to them all eventually, but we'll have to be careful how we play it. I don't want to scare the murderer off."

We sat in silence for the rest of the drive, each busy with our own thoughts, and when we got back to the police station I handed Alec my notebook so he could go through it. I already had a pretty good idea of its contents—my memory wasn't bad—so I intended to do a bit of thinking of my own. I decided to go and get a cup of tea in the little tea shop across the road and mull things over.

I hadn't been into the tea room before, and I was pleasantly surprised. It was a charming little shop with a warm, welcoming atmosphere and an appetising selection of homemade cakes on display. I treated myself to a cup of tea and a scone, and took a seat by the window, thinking about the interview.

Peter Maloney had admitted to seeing Brian that night and getting into some sort of altercation, but he'd sworn he was home shortly afterwards. But there was something in his eyes when he said it that had convinced me his story wasn't entirely true, and Grace hadn't been around to verify it one way or the other, so where had she been? What was really going on with the railway line extension? And was any of it connected to the ghost train? My head was beginning to ache with all the questions, but I thought we needed to speak to Grace Maloney next. Maybe she could shed some light on her husband's activities.

Oddly enough, as if my thoughts had summoned her, the bell over the door tinkled and Grace entered the shop, accompanied by Edith, Jessie and Esme. I wondered if she ever went anywhere alone. They took a seat at a table across from mine and placed their orders. There was no one else in the shop, and the weight of propriety was apparently heavy on Jessie, for she leaned across and asked, "Would you like to join us, Mrs Adams?" I caught the glances the others, especially Grace and Esme, threw at her, clearly admonishing this display of sociability, but the words couldn't be taken back.

"Why, yes, thank you," I said, moving my chair over to their table. I didn't particularly want to sit with them, but these ladies had proved to be one of the most reliable sources of news in town and, given how stuck we were at the moment, I'd take all the leads I could get.

"I hear you're working with Constable Ward to investigate Mr Mathieson's murder," Jessie said, eyes wide, and I realised now why she was so keen to have me sit with them. Gossip went both ways, and this piece had travelled fast.

"That's right, but I'm just a scribe. I don't have any role in the investigation itself." Let them believe they could trust me.

"It must be thrilling!"

"Not really—just lots of talking to people."

"Are you going to be interviewing us?" She looked so keen I nearly smiled, but I managed to hold it in. Did she think we *needed* to be interviewing them?

"Well, the constable is talking to all sorts of people at the moment. He's just trying to figure out where Mr Mathieson went that evening." Or, more importantly, who came to him.

"Oh," Jessie said, sounding a little disappointed. "Well, I never really met the man, I'm afraid. And I was home all night with James." She seemed a bit wistful, as if she wished she could have had a bigger part in the most exciting thing to hit the town since the railway accident all those years ago.

"Me too," Edith added, clearly not wanting to be left out. "I was home with David all night."

Grace and Esme said nothing, and I began to wonder. If Jessie and Edith were home it clearly wasn't a Ladies' Auxiliary meeting that took Grace out that night, for all of them would be in groups like that together. So it must have been something far more personal—but what? Now wasn't the time to ask, but I made a mental note to tell Alec.

"Will you be joining us for dinner at the Andersons' tomorrow, Mrs Adams?" Edith asked. Grace shot her a look, but she either failed to intercept it or ignored it. I found it funny that Grace's underlings suddenly seemed to have taken to me, clearly much to her chagrin. But this was the first I'd heard of such a dinner.

"No, unfortunately," I said, "for I've not been invited by Mrs Anderson."

"Oh no," Jessie said, "that can't be right. I'll let Mary know. I'm sure she'll be happy to extend the invitation to you. It will even up the numbers, for Father Sam is also coming and I don't believe he has a companion, as Esme is unable to attend."

"Thank you. It sounds lovely. But I'm not yet acquainted with Mrs Anderson."

"Oh, you'll love her, don't worry. She's the most generous soul. We all dine there quite frequently."

"Are the Andersons well-liked in Tungold?"

"Yes, of course. John is our longest-serving mayor."

All this time I'd been watching Grace out of the corner of my eye; her lips were getting thinner and thinner and it was clear she didn't share Jessie's enthusiasm for either my attendance at the dinner or the Andersons in general. I supposed this came from her husband's opposition to the line extension, not to mention the rather rude comments John had made about Matthew Maloney at the dance.

The little gathering broke up shortly afterwards, with an agreement to meet at the Carters' the following evening to travel to the Andersons' together. Jessie assured me that I didn't need to wait for a formal invitation from Mrs Anderson, although this left me feeling a bit awkward. I wasn't usually one to stand on ceremony, but Ma had managed to drill some basic manners into me, so the idea of just turning up made me uncomfortable. But I didn't want to pass up the chance to further ingratiate myself into Tungold society, and hopefully glean a few more pieces of information at the same time.

I didn't tell Alec I was going to the dinner—partly because I didn't bump into him, but mainly because I wanted to pursue this line of enquiry myself. I also felt a little bad that he hadn't been invited, and I didn't want to rub it in. I'd tell him if anything significant arose as a result, but otherwise it would just be a nice night out. And I didn't want to go there feeling like he was looking over my shoulder all the time, especially as I wasn't really convinced right now about his powers of deduction.

I wandered home in the golden afternoon light, musing on all that had occurred. I wasn't quite sure what to make of it all.

When I reached my verandah I noticed a large wooden box sitting before the front door. A closer inspection revealed a label with my name on it and I stared at it, intrigued. I never received parcels, for the only person who sent me mail was Lottie, and she couldn't afford extravagances. The lid seemed to be quite loosely fitted, and I wondered if someone had been prying, perhaps at the station. With an excited thrill I lifted it off, although a surge of puzzlement enveloped me at a strange hissing noise that arose from within.

I peered into the box, then recoiled in horror, letting out a scream in spite of myself. Coiled around each other in the crate were two snakes, dark brown and as thick as my forearm. One was raised to strike, showing me its creamy underbelly. I flung the lid back on the crate, not waiting to see if it landed true, and ran as fast as I could back up the path, out the gate and into the road. Terror gave power to my legs, and I didn't stop running until I saw the pub looming up before me in the main street.

There weren't many people around now, but I still had the presence of mind to slow to a fast walk and try to calm my breathing. I didn't want to make a scene or let whoever left those vile creatures there know they'd rattled me. But my hands were shaking and my mind was racing so fast that I could barely think straight. Before I knew it, I found myself on the steps of the police station.

Alec responded to my insistent knocking in his shirt-sleeves—he must have been preparing his dinner. "Jane?" he asked in alarm when he saw me. "What's wrong?" I wondered for a second how he knew, then I realised I must look a wreck, with my hair flung everywhere and dust from the road sticking to the sweat on my face.

I was still slightly hysterical from the shock, but I managed to babble out something relatively coherent. Still, Alec sounded slightly sceptical.

"Someone sent you a box of snakes? Why on earth would they do that?"

"I think it's because I was asking questions about the ghost train." Of course, he then asked what had drawn me to that conclusion, so I reluctantly told him about Bertha.

"You should have come to me earlier."

"I didn't want to make a fuss. And it seemed ridiculous."

"Never mind," he said, pulling on his coat. "Let's go and deal with these beasties then, shall we?"

Dealing with the snakes was the last thing I wanted to do—they were the one thing that truly terrified me—and my stomach twisted in apprehension as Alec harnessed the horse to the trap. We could easily have walked, but my knees were still trembling and I was grateful that I didn't have to.

When we reached my house Alec parked right outside the gate. "Stay here," he commanded, and for once I had no wish to argue with him. The box was still on the verandah, the lid slightly ajar. Alec picked up a long branch from the garden and climbed the steps. Carefully, he used the branch to lever the lid off the box, then hurried back down the path. I watched intently from the safety of the trap. At first nothing happened, and I began to wonder if I'd dreamed the whole thing. What on earth would Alec think if the crate turned out to be empty? But then slowly, sinuously, a dark shape draped itself over the edge of the box and slid silkily to the ground.

The first snake was quickly followed by the other, and I slowly unclenched my hands as they slithered through the garden and away towards the bush on the far side of the road.

I was unprepared for the wave of relief that washed over me, and I had to press my lips together to hold back an unexpected sob. I had no doubt that this was all connected to the ghost train, and whoever was behind it clearly meant business.

"Would you like a cup of tea?" I asked Alec as he helped me down from the trap. Now that the danger had passed, I was a bit angry with myself that I'd needed rescuing. I took great pride in being able to stand on my own two feet, and that pride had taken a beating this afternoon.

"Thank you," he said, following me into the house.

I stoked the fire and set the kettle to boil. "Milk and sugar?"

"Both, please. I'd say someone really has it in for you," he added, sitting down at the table. "What have you done?"

I rather resented the implication that I'd *done* anything, but I tried not to let it show. "Nothing—I just asked a few questions about the ghost train, like I told you. They're just trying to warn me off."

"Are you sure that's all they're trying to do?"

"What are you suggesting?" I asked, putting a cup in front of him and pouring the tea.

"Well, Brian Mathieson was looking into the line extension, and he got himself pushed off a balcony. You've been asking questions about the ghost train, and someone clearly doesn't like it. I hate to say it, but what if the 'J.A. murder' in the note Brian left before he died referred not to John Anderson, but to you?"

"Surely not! You think I could be next?"

"I think it's a possibility, and until Brian's killer is caught, we have to take every precaution. Keep your doors and windows locked and if you see anything suspicious you telephone me immediately, you understand? I'd rather you wake me in the middle of the night than have something happen to you." He smiled at me rather tenderly as he said this, and I couldn't help but feel a pleasant flutter in my chest.

"I'm not allowed to use the telephone for personal calls."

"I'm sure even Mr Bailey would make an exception in these circumstances."

"Perhaps." I wasn't so sure, but I let it go.

We talked of other things for a while, sipping our tea, and the afternoon's horrors began to recede. At last Alec rose reluctantly.

"I should be going," he said. "Thank you for the tea."

"It's I who should be thanking you," I said. "I really appreciate your help."

"My pleasure," he said. "You take care, Jane." He squeezed my hand, then unexpectedly brushed it with his lips. A thrill tingled down my spine, and I wondered for a moment what it would be like to kiss him.

"Good night, Alec."

CHAPTER 10

The next day I had no real plans except dinner at the Andersons' in the evening, so I decided to hunt down Alec again and see if he'd had any blinding insights into the investigation overnight. I wondered whether to tell him my suspicions about Grace, and how I was sure she was hiding something. Really, if I found anyone in this town who was prepared to be entirely honest I thought I'd probably drop dead from the shock of it.

I found Alec at his desk in the police station. On one wall a large piece of paper was tacked up, on which he seemed to be building some sort of timeline. Peter's reported movements were there, and the estimated time of Brian's death, but other than that it looked conspicuously empty.

"How did you go with my notes?" I asked.

He shrugged. "We don't really have much to go on, do we?"

"Not yet. But we'll get there." I paused. "I think we should interview Grace Maloney."

"Grace? Why?"

"There was no Ladies' Auxiliary meeting on that night, so I want to know where she was."

"You think a *woman* killed Brian?"

"Why not? It's just as plausible as a man, surely."

"But...he wasn't a small man. I doubt she would have been able to overpower him like that."

I shrugged. "Maybe. But it's still worth a try, don't you think? I mean, do we have anything else to go on?"

"Not really. Do you want to go and see her now?"

I thought about the dinner that night, and how much easier it would be for me to get information if we hadn't already put Grace on her guard. "No, not yet. Let's do it tomorrow."

"I doubt we'll get much from her."

"Well, what else do you suggest?"

"I think we should go and see Doctor Carter. He should have finished his examination of the body by now, and he might be able to tell us something."

David Carter's surgery wasn't far from the church—perhaps so that his failures could be quickly dispatched. As well as the office where he saw his living patients, there was a small stone building set off to one side, which was a morgue of sorts. Alec told me it wasn't often used for post-mortems—they didn't get many suspicious deaths round here.

We ignored the morgue for the time being and walked into the surgery. I was surprised to see Edith seated behind a desk in the waiting area, until I realised that she must be her husband's secretary. There was no one else in the waiting room. Incongruously, a stuffed possum glared down at us, glassy-eyed, from the mantelpiece, staring into the middle distance. A cockatoo sat next to it, its yellow crest permanently raised. I shuddered and turned away.

"Good morning," Edith said. "Have you come to see the doctor?"

"Yes, thank you," Alec said. "Official business. Could you please tell him we're here?"

"Certainly." She knocked on the door then opened it and stuck her head inside. "Constable Ward and Mrs Adams." Turning back to us, she said, "You can go in."

I'd never liked doctors' offices, and I was glad I wasn't here as a patient. But Alec seemed unfazed by the rather grim surroundings, and he just marched on in as if he did this every day.

Dr Carter was a tall, rather handsome man of around fifty. He probably would have been called dashing when he was younger, and he hadn't yet gone entirely to seed. His dark hair and moustache were peppered with grey, but his bearing as he stood to greet us implied utter self-confidence. I found it odd that he was married to such a little mouse as Edith, but then I supposed there was only room for one strong personality in such a union. I guessed she looked after him and in return he gave her a sense of security. There were worse bases for a marriage. I should know.

"Constable," he said. "You've come about Brian Mathieson, I suppose?"

"That's right," Alec said. "Have you finished your examination?"

"I have. Care to see for yourself?" He led the way out of the office without waiting for a response, and Alec and I followed. We headed over to the morgue, and I could smell it before we even got close. My stomach fluttered.

"Perhaps it would be better if you wait outside, Mrs Adams?" the doctor suggested. I wasn't normally squeamish, but this time I couldn't help but agree. I hoped Alec didn't think me weak.

The smell of chemicals and death was making me lightheaded, so I returned to the surgery. Edith was still there, filing papers.

"What...charming ornaments," I said, gesturing to the stuffed possum and cockatoo in an attempt to make conversation. In truth, I didn't find them particularly charming; they gave me the willies.

"Thank you," Edith beamed. "I stuffed them myself. Taxidermy is my passion."

"*Really?*" I asked, intrigued. I would never have thought that meek little Edith would go in for something quite so ghoulish.

"Oh yes. I'm self-taught and not very good at it yet, but I've been fascinated by it ever since I saw pictures of Mr Hancock's work from the Great Exhibition when I was just a girl."

I smiled rather fixedly, pretending that I knew what she was talking about. "Are these the only ones you've done?"

"Oh no, I've got half a dozen more. Wait a minute and I'll show you." She bustled out of the office, returning five minutes later carrying a crimson rosella mounted on a plinth.

"This is my most recent one."

"It's beautiful," I said, although in truth I found something deeply sad about seeing the little red and blue parrot captured so. "You've got a real talent."

"Thank you."

Unsure of what to say next, I scuffed the toe of my boot awkwardly on a pattern in the carpet, but I was thankfully spared from further contemplation of the taxidermist's art by Dr Carter's voice drifting down the hallway as the men returned from the morgue.

"I've spoken to Father Allsop, and the funeral will be tomorrow," he was saying. "Mr Mathieson doesn't seem to have had any family that we can track down, and he really needs to be interred as soon as possible, as you saw. Unlike a fine wine, bodies tend not to improve with age."

"I think a quick burial is a good idea," Alec said as they entered the waiting room. "And we can keep a close eye on who turns up."

"You really think the murderer will come to the funeral?" I asked as we walked back to the police station. "Surely that's pretty callous, even for someone like that."

Alec shrugged. "I don't know. But I imagine half the town will be there. These sorts of things—births, deaths, marriages—are social occasions in a place like this, and I'd like to see how different people react. You never know, we may get some sort of lead, and at the moment I'll take whatever we can get."

We went our separate ways after that, promising to meet at the funeral the next day. I needed to prepare for dinner that evening, for I didn't often get invited to formal events and wanted to make sure I looked my best. I'd even decided to wash my hair, for it was a sunny day and hopefully it wouldn't take too long to dry it.

My toilette, I'm ashamed to say, took up most of the afternoon. I wasn't normally one to engage in such womanly pursuits, but there was something special about getting all dressed up, even though the only 'fancy' gown I owned was the lavender silk I'd worn to the dance. I also had some paste jewellery that Lottie had given me at Jim's funeral—a strange choice of gift, but perhaps something that showed she understood more than she let on. I really should write to her, for it had been several weeks since we last corresponded.

Standing before the looking glass in my bedroom, I was pleased with what I saw. My shoes were just my everyday ones, but the gown was long enough to hide them, and in any case I could hardly walk all the way into town in dainty little slippers. I'd even managed to dress my hair in a way that, while not ornate, was quite becoming. I felt the ladies ought to be pleasantly surprised.

I left in plenty of time so as not to have to rush, for the last thing I wanted was to arrive in town sweaty and bedraggled. Even so, when I reached the Carters' house I was the last one of the group. The other ladies were ready in the parlour, sipping tea out of dainty china cups and twittering like little birds. They looked up when the maid showed me in, and I wondered if they'd been talking about me. I got the feeling that Grace in particular was unhappy that I was to be a member of their party tonight.

"Have you been to Ellery before, Mrs Adams?" Jessie Brown asked after we'd exchanged greetings.

"No," I said, wondering if I should let on that I had no idea what she was talking about.

"I suppose you don't move in these circles very often," Grace said, raising an eyebrow.

"But I'm sure you'll like it," Jessie said hurriedly. "It's one of the finest houses in the district, apart from Queensgrace, of course."

"Of course."

"It was nice to see you this morning," Edith chipped in, with apparent sincerity. "How goes the investigation?"

I shrugged noncommittally, unsure of how much I should say, but thankfully these women flitted about like sparrows, pre-empting my reply. Grace had turned away, apparently bored by our conversation.

"It must be all rather thrilling," Jessie said, who seemed to have a morbid fascination with Brian's murder that wasn't entirely proper. I liked her slightly more for it.

"I suppose so..." I didn't really know how to respond to this. "I mean, it's an awful event, but I'm glad I can help. I daresay we'll be visiting Ellery soon too."

"You surely don't think Mr Anderson had anything to do with it, do you?" Edith said. "He's one of the nicest men in the district."

"Don't let Grace's husband hear you say that," Jessie said with a grin, glancing across at her friend. But Grace had crossed the room to discuss something with the maid and didn't appear to have heard.

"We're just pursuing all lines of enquiry," I said, amused by how official I sounded, as if I was more than just a simple scribe. "We have to look at everything, you know."

"Oh yes, I understand," Jessie said. "You can't let someone get away with *murder*." Her eyes widened, and I wanted to smile at her innocence. She was a sweet woman, but not exactly dazzling in her brilliance. It was probably why Grace got on with her so well. Grace liked people she could manipulate.

The object of my thoughts turned at this point and walked over to us. Although her companions seemed to have warmed to me a little, she was still as cold and standoffish as ever.

"Well, this is a jolly group," she said, although her eyes said something different. Grace was one of those people who could smile with her mouth while her eyes remained absolutely cold.

"What time are we expected at Ellery?" I asked, for the afternoon was drawing to a close.

"We should be going," Grace said. "We were just waiting for you. The men will be meeting us there." *Of course* our tardiness was my fault.

We put on our hats and went outside to where the Carters' manservant was waiting. He helped us into the tray of the large cart, then hoisted himself up and clicked to the horses. We sat on the bench seats that had been fitted into the bed of the cart, and which actually weren't too uncomfortable. It reminded me of the hay rides my brothers and sister and I used to go on in Goulburn as children. Part of me wished I was back there, in my childhood, carefree, instead of stuck here in this town with a dead railway official, a coterie of women who disliked me, and a mysterious adversary who wished me harm. But here I was, as Ma would say, with nought to do but make the best of it.

Dust hung suspended in the dry, still air as the cart bumbled and jolted through town, out the opposite end to my cottage, along a way I hadn't been before. I didn't really feel like talking, so I just sat and listened to the ladies gossiping about idle subjects. I wondered how I could get Grace to confess to where she really was the night Brian died. Maybe I should lean on Edith or Jessie a bit instead. They were much less worldly and much more inclined to talk.

We reached a rise near the top of the escarpment and saw the beautiful pastoral country stretching out below us, bathed in golden late-afternoon light. Whenever I saw country like this I wondered how Ma could still pine so much for Ireland. No green and pleasant land for me; I liked the wildness of the bush. Maybe that was why we could never quite see eye-to-eye.

Ellery turned out to be a large house—for the district—set in one of the leafy back streets of town. Unlike most of the cottages in Tungold, which were weatherboard, this house was made of stone. It wasn't as ostentatious as Queensgrace, but I liked it more on first impressions—as it rose before us in the twilight, all beautifully lit and glowing, it had a cosy, welcoming feeling about it. Lanterns hung from the verandah posts as swallows swooped among the eaves. It was clearly the best house in town, fitting for the mayor and his wife.

A woman, who I presumed was Mary Anderson, came out to greet us as the cart pulled to a stop. The manservant helped us down and then handed the horse's reins to a stableboy who appeared from somewhere around the back.

Together they led the horse and cart away, leaving us standing in the driveway.

"Well now, this is a pleasure!" Mrs Anderson said. "It's been too long! Please, come inside." Now that the sun had dipped below the tree line, the evening had grown unexpectedly cool, so I was all too ready to accept her invitation. As we walked in—Grace first with Mrs Anderson, then Edith and Jessie, and me last—I took the opportunity to study our hostess. Mary Anderson was about Grace's age, with an open, pleasant face full of smile lines, and a comfortably plump figure. She looked like the very idea of someone's mother. I didn't know how many children she had, but I imagined she was a tough, capable woman—these country matrons always were. You had to be to survive out here.

Only once we were in the hallway taking off our hats did she notice me lurking at the back of the group. "Mrs Adams, I presume?" she asked, coming forward and grasping my hand cordially in her own. "It's such a pleasure to finally meet you."

"Likewise, and thank you for having me."

"You're very welcome, my dear."

I was already warming to Mary Anderson, and I wondered if she knew about the note that Alec had discovered and its possible reference to her husband. But I decided that I didn't want to worry her at this stage. Better to discuss it with Mr Anderson himself at another time.

"Have our menfolk arrived?" Edith asked as we were led through to a cosy parlour.

"Not yet," Mary said, "but I daresay they shan't be long. My John is only just back from Sydney Town himself, so he'll be joining us too." All the others—except Grace, of course—looked pleased at this news, but I hoped it wouldn't be as deathly dull as it sounded: a roomful of old married couples, a priest and me. I reminded myself that I was here for information. This was work, not pleasure.

There was the sound of horses on the gravel driveway and the women looked up. In a few moments the door to the parlour opened and the maid showed in Dr Carter, Mr Brown and Father Allsop. I wondered where Peter Maloney was, but it was quickly explained.

"I must apologise on behalf of our friend," Dr Carter said, going over to Mrs Anderson. "He had a matter of urgent business that could not be delayed, and I'm afraid he'll be unable to join us tonight." I glanced over at Grace and caught her thunderous expression. I had the distinct impression that she didn't believe the 'urgent business' excuse for a second, but then her mask dropped and she again appeared impassive. I wondered if Peter had deliberately made up a pretext for his absence so he didn't have to face John Anderson. I suspected there would be some heated discussions at Queensgrace later.

A maid came in at this point and announced that dinner was served, and I was grateful, for my stomach was rumbling. We were shown into a large, comfortable dining room, whose centrepiece was a beautiful mahogany table, big enough to seat us all with ease. I found myself positioned between Mr Brown and Father Allsop. The soup arrived and Mr Brown turned immediately to his right-hand neighbour, Grace Maloney, engaging her in conversation and leaving me to entertain the elderly priest.

"Have you had a good day, Father?" I asked in an effort to make small talk.

"What? Oh yes, quite." I knew him only by sight, but now did not appear the time to deepen our acquaintance; he seemed vague and distracted.

"Lovely weather we're having, isn't it?"

He looked at me like I was mad. "It's rather hot for my taste, I'm afraid." Clearly deciding that conversation with me was not worth pursuing, he turned to Mrs Anderson, who was sitting at the foot of the table, to his left, and I returned awkwardly to my food.

My two companions steadfastly ignored me throughout the first course, so I rose and excused myself. When I returned to the table Dr Carter was also absent; perhaps he was finding the conversation tedious too.

We had just finished the soup when the door opened and John Anderson entered. Mrs Anderson beamed, and the overall mood in the room lightened with the entrance of the host.

"My apologies, everyone," he said. "I've only just returned, and I had to take care of some pressing business. Delightful to see you all." He took his place at the head of the table and the maid brought his soup. Grace was sitting to his left, Edith to his right, and he immediately turned his charm on the two women. Even the frosty Mrs Maloney practically melted under his words.

I confess I felt a bit let down by the whole party, given how eagerly I'd anticipated it. Mary Anderson was a friendly and welcoming hostess, but the calibre of my fellow diners was sadly lacking. I'd never been one for highfalutin conversation, but a little acknowledgement would have been nice.

After dinner, the ladies retired to the drawing room while the gentlemen went for port and cigars. Although I hadn't been to all that many dinner parties, I'd always found this to be a strange custom. The ladies' conversation was invariably full of frills and frippery, and I couldn't help wishing I could have stayed with the men and talked business and farming and politics. Those sorts of things had always been of much more interest to me than the fluff my sex was supposed to prefer. One of the things I liked about Alec was that he never treated me as just a girl, the way these men seemed to.

"How are you liking Tungold, Jane?" Mary Anderson asked as we sipped our tea.

"Very well, thank you." I figured it was prudent to be polite.

"And you're the new level crossing gatekeeper?"

"That's right."

"You were widowed quite recently, weren't you?" Grace dropped in. "*Such* a tragedy."

I didn't really know what to say to this. Of course she knew I was a widow, and I wasn't sure what her intentions were. "Yes, it was."

"Mary," Jessie called from the table by the window where she was sitting with Edith, "we were just talking about your exquisite embroidery. Won't you show us your latest work?"

"Excuse me," Mary said, rising with a smile.

"It must be *very difficult* for you without your husband here," Grace continued, once we were alone.

"I manage."

"I noticed Constable Ward has been assisting you." Ah. So *that* was what she was up to. I felt my cheeks beginning to burn, and I knew that now that she had me squirming she wasn't going to let me go easily.

"He's been very kind, yes. A good friend."

"He couldn't take his eyes off you at the dance."

"I'm sure that wasn't the case." Secretly, I was actually a little flattered, which probably wasn't what she had intended.

"And Jessie said she saw him working in your garden." She threw it at me like an accusation.

"That's no crime."

She gave a glittering laugh. "Of course not. I'm just trying to *warn* you, as your *friend*. This is a small town and people may talk."

"It sounds like they already are."

"We only have your interests at heart, dear Jane. After all, I'm *sure* you have a reputation to protect." She made it sound like a threat.

There were many things I wanted to say to the vicious old gossip, but I was conscious that it wouldn't be wise to make an enemy of her, and I wasn't exactly at home here; not yet. Thankfully, though, I was spared any further humiliation by Jessie.

"Grace, dear, come and look at this stitching. We *must* have this piece for the next Art Society exhibition!"

"Excuse me," Grace said, leaving me nursing my bruises on the chaise longue. I felt like I'd just been in a fight, and now that it was done there was a rather painful lump in my throat. My heart was still racing.

None of them talked to me for the rest of the evening. Mary did shoot sympathetic glances my way from time to time, but whenever she attempted to come over and fulfil her hostess duties, one of the others had some immediate need of her presence. In the end I chose a volume of Longfellow's poetry from the small bookcase and read, ignoring them as best I could.

It wasn't a late night, and I was glad. They even dropped me off at my cottage to save me having to walk back alone in the dark, the one kind gesture they'd made to me all evening. In my room I flung my hat and wrap onto the bed, then sank to the floor, head in my hands. It was clear now that the ladies had only invited me in order to humiliate me, and I cursed myself for not seeing it earlier. I'd been so pleased to think that I was finally finding a place in Tungold society that I'd completely underestimated them. In spite of myself I couldn't help shedding a few bitter tears. And I hadn't even got any decent information out of the whole exercise. Peter Maloney was still free as a bird.

CHAPTER II

The next morning the weather was grey and overcast, just right for a funeral; it wasn't raining, but cheerful sunlight would somehow have seemed wrong. At least this had the appropriate air of mourning. As Alec had anticipated, half the town appeared to have turned out for the occasion, and the church was nearly full. I found this odd, given how little time they'd had for Brian while he was alive. But I supposed people in small towns liked an event, so at least he'd given them some happiness in death, if not in life.

As I took my seat in a middle pew I realised that the circumstances of Brian's death had probably also drawn people out; the opportunity for gossip was just too good to pass up. They couldn't talk too openly, of course—for Father Allsop was patrolling and shooting grim looks if they appeared to be enjoying themselves too much—but I sat and listened to the whispers. It was all idle speculation, and I didn't hear anything I didn't already know. If the killer was here, he was keeping mum.

I'd been to funerals before—Jim's, of course, and that of a young girl I knew from school who'd died of consumption—but this was by far the oddest I'd ever attended. There was no family present, and no one who seemed to know the deceased particularly well or think highly of him. Thus the eulogy was short and the sermon long, and I found my mind beginning to wander. Part of me almost felt sorry for Brian, having such a send-off, but then I remembered what sort of man he'd been and my compassion dissipated. His death reflected the way he'd lived; as far as I was concerned, he'd brought it on himself.

Alec was sitting down the front, too far away for me to catch his eye. There were other familiar faces in the crowd: Annie Graham, Polly and Stan, Esme Johnson, the Maloneys, the Carters and the Browns, as well as some I didn't know. Charlie Chin was there, in normal clothes this time, and I was guessing the others came from farms around the district. But I didn't see the Andersons there, which struck me as odd, especially since John Anderson seemed to be the only person in town who had had any time for Brian at all.

We sang a final hymn and the pallbearers carried the coffin out and across to the little graveyard. The grave had already been dug, and the coffin was lowered and dirt thrown with little ceremony other than the prayers. There was no headstone, just a simple wooden cross with Brian's name and the dates of his birth and death, and I surmised that there was nobody to pay for a proper one. It looked bare and stark next to its ornate sandstone neighbours.

The church ladies, bless them, had put on a kind of wake in the hall, although I suspected it was less about remembering Brian than it was about a social gathering. In any case, over tea and biscuits, the gossip started in earnest. I turned to find Alec at my elbow, looking unusually serious.

"Is everything all right?" I asked, suddenly worried, although I couldn't explain why.

He shook his head, taking my arm and drawing me into a corner where we were less likely to be overhead. "Not really. John Anderson was poisoned last night."

"What?" He'd looked fine when I'd seen him at dinner. "When? How?"

"I don't know." He rubbed his eyes tiredly. "But a messenger came from Ellery this morning. He's gravely ill."

"How do they know it was poison? It could have just been the food."

"Apparently he ate exactly the same thing as the rest of you at the dinner party and nobody else got sick," he said. I half-expected him to berate me for not telling him about the dinner, but he didn't. "He was the last person to be served, so they fed some of the leftovers to one of the dogs as a test. The dog died."

"I can't believe it." I didn't know what to make of this. The poor dog.

"I'm afraid it's true."

"So Brian was right, then."

"What do you mean?"

"Well, that note that you found. *J.A. murder*. It wasn't about me at all. He must have known someone would try to kill John Anderson."

"But why?"

"It must be something to do with the railway, surely. I mean, everything points back to that. So that would make Peter Maloney the obvious suspect, as if he wasn't already."

Alec glanced over his shoulder. "I don't think we should discuss this here."

"You're right. But just think about it. It all fits."

"We'll talk about this later."

"You know I'm right."

"I know I want evidence."

I shrugged. I was confident he'd come around to my way of seeing things.

After the wake I went over to the police station to continue our conversation. I'd been considering all morning how to convince Alec, but it turned out he was halfway there already.

"I've been thinking about what you said," he said. "It's clear Peter Maloney isn't telling us the whole truth. But it's a big leap to then accuse him of attempted murder."

"What if it wasn't him?"

"But you were just insisting it was!"

"No, what I mean is, what if it wasn't *only* him? What if it's a conspiracy?"

"A conspiracy? In Tungold?" His tone was one of disbelief, and I couldn't really blame him. A town like this wasn't the place you'd expect to find a criminal gang. These people organised dances, not conspiracies.

"I've been thinking about it," I said. "Peter wasn't at the dinner party last night, so he didn't really have any opportunity. But Doctor Carter was, and so was Father Allsop. Either of them could have done it."

"The *doctor* or the *priest?*"

"Even doctors and priests can be bad people," I said. I thought of the ones I'd known over the years and shuddered. "A person's job doesn't suddenly grant them sainthood."

"No, of course not. That's not what I meant. But really, why would either of them do such a thing?"

"Well, Doctor Carter is a chum of Peter Maloney's, and he's as much against the railway extension as Peter is," I said. "He's not as openly vocal about it, but I've heard them talking together. That would give them both a motive for murdering Brian *and* Mr Anderson. Plus, he's a doctor—he'd have access to all sorts of medicines and potions, some of them poisonous if the dose is high enough. *And* he was absent from the table for a while last night—long enough to slip something into the food."

"It's all entirely circumstantial."

"We haven't talked to him yet about where he was the night Brian died, though, have we? We've always just assumed he was innocent."

Alec inclined his head in concession to this. "You're right. I suppose we should pay the good doctor another visit."

I expected Dr Carter to be out on house calls when we visited, but to my surprise his buggy drew up just as we approached the surgery.

"Constable Ward," he said, jumping down and shaking Alec's hand. "I was just about to call on you. I've just come from Ellery."

"Not bad news, I hope?"

"Not good, but not as bad as it could be," he said. "Mr Anderson is still very ill, but I believe the worst is over. I think he should make a full recovery, in time."

"I'm very glad to hear it, Doctor. I was worried I'd have another murder enquiry on my hands."

"Not today, thank God."

"Any idea what he was poisoned with?"

Dr Carter shook his head. "It's impossible to tell. Some sort of fast-acting drug, I'd say, but I really don't know at this stage. But I'm pretty sure it was deliberate."

"I'll be heading out to Ellery this afternoon," Alec said. "Do you think he'll be up to talking?"

"Probably not today, but all the staff are there. You can ask them what happened, not that it'll do you much good, I fear. The maids are all over the place. They clearly love the man and I can't see that any of them would have done anything to hurt him."

"Well, you never know."

"That's true enough. Now, was there something I could help you with?"

"May we go inside? I've just got a few questions."

"Ah, ruling me out as a suspect, eh?" He grinned jovially, but there was something else in his eyes. If I didn't know better, I'd have said it was fear.

Dr Carter unlocked the surgery door and we went into his office. Edith was nowhere to be seen. He took a seat behind the desk, ushering us to chairs in front.

"Tell me, Doctor, where were you the night Brian died?"

The doctor looked unexpectedly shifty. "I was out. On a house call."

"To whom?"

"That's confidential, Constable."

"I don't wish to know the medical details, just to whom I can speak for confirmation."

"I'm afraid I can't give you that information."

"Then I'm afraid I must list you as a suspect."

"That's ridiculous!"

"If I can't verify your alibi, I have no choice."

Despite having only just sat down, Dr Carter rose to his feet, his expression like granite. "I think you'd better go now. You said you needed to visit Ellery."

"Quite," Alec said, also rising. I followed suit. "But I suggest you speak to your patient and arrange for him to confirm your whereabouts. We wouldn't want any misunderstandings."

"Indeed we wouldn't. You can show yourselves out?"

"Of course."

We left, closing the study door on the still-fuming doctor. I wondered if Alec was wise to be so heavy-handed, but he was clearly starting to feel frustrated about being blocked at every turn: first Peter Maloney, now Dr Carter.

"Don't say 'I told you so'," he said as we walked out into the sticky summer air. The sun was struggling valiantly to break through the clouds, and the day was muggy.

"I wouldn't dream of it. It's suspicious, though, isn't it?"

"Looks that way. Fancy a drive to Ellery?"

"Love to."

When we arrived at the house it had a different air to the night before—gone was the gaiety, replaced by a sombre silence. The maid who answered the door looked worn out, her eyes red-rimmed and puffy. She showed us to the parlour and went to fetch Mrs Anderson.

I'd noticed over the years that most women, when confronted with a crisis, fitted into one of two camps. They either fell apart completely, descended into hysterics and took to their beds, being of no use to anyone, or they pursed their lips, raised their chins and simply got on with doing what needed to be done. It was immediately obvious that Mary Anderson was one of the latter. There were shadows under her eyes, but she was well-dressed and carried herself with quiet dignity. Despite her obvious worry for her husband, she poured us tea and was in all aspects the perfect hostess. I admired her fortitude.

"You must forgive me, Constable," she said. "I've had little sleep."

"Of course, ma'am. How is Mr Anderson?"

"Doctor Carter says he'll live, although he may take some time to recover," she said. "He's sleeping at present. But I just thank the Lord it wasn't fatal. Who could possibly do such a thing? John is a good man." Tears sprang to her eyes, but she blinked them away. I reached over and patted her hand, and she gave me a watery smile.

"Does your husband have any enemies?" Alec asked.

"Enemies? No," Mary said. "I mean, there are some people who object to his views on the railway, but surely they wouldn't do something like this!" She looked horrified at the thought.

"What about the servants?"

"No, not at all. He's a good master and they all love him. He's fair and he pays them well. I can barely remember any disputes, let alone one that would end in someone trying to kill him!"

"And have you had any unexpected visitors? Any swaggies or anyone dropping by?"

"No, not lately. If any tramps come through we occasionally let them bunk down in the stable, but I haven't seen one for months. And why would a swaggy want to poison John?"

"I'm just trying to rule everything out, Mrs Anderson. Now, can you take me through exactly what happened last night?"

"Well, we had a little dinner party. You were there, Mrs Adams, and of course the Carters, the Browns, Father Allsop and Mrs Maloney. Mr Maloney was also invited but he was called away at the last minute on urgent business."

"And your husband had just returned from Sydney, is that correct?"

"Yes. He came home just before the guests arrived, but he had a few matters to see to first, so he was late for dinner."

"So he ate after everyone else?"

"Yes."

"And he never left the table?"

"No."

"Did any of the other guests?"

"Dr Carter and Mrs Adams both needed to...refresh themselves...during the evening."

"Was that before or after Mr Anderson arrived?"

"Uh...I don't know..." Mrs Anderson blushed.

"Before," I said.

"Thank you."

"And who prepares the food?"

"The cook and the kitchen maids."

"I'll need to talk to them too."

"Of course."

Unfortunately, the cook and the maids had little to offer us. There were three of them and they were all distraught.

"I have no idea how it could have happened," the cook, Mrs Jenkins, said, sobbing into her handkerchief. "I never saw no one put nothing into the food. But we were that busy in here that night. It were just me and Bessie, for Flora was took to her bed sick with a headache."

"I was asleep the whole time," the unfortunate Flora said, her lip trembling. She was clearly terrified we were about to label her a killer and haul her off to gaol. "I swear, I never left my room."

"Did anyone come into the kitchen during the evening?"

"Not that I saw," Bessie, the other maid said. "But like Mrs Jenkins says, we were that busy, and I had to wait on the table too."

"Was there any point where both of you were out of the room?"

The two of them contemplated the question for a moment.

"Just a couple of minutes," Mrs Jenkins said. "Bessie was serving and I had to pop into the larder to get something. It's a big larder—you have to walk right in. But I was only in there for a minute."

"Long enough for someone to sneak in and put something in the food?"

"I wouldn't have thought so, sir, but yes, I suppose."

There was a silence while we all mulled over this possibility.

"Do you enjoy working for the Andersons?" Alec asked.

"Oh, yes, sir," Bessie said, and the other two nodded in agreement. "I was so lucky to get this position, and I wouldn't want to work anywhere else. They treat us all real well and they're a right fine family."

"Couldn't have put it better myself," Mrs Jenkins said, although she seemed determined to try. "They respect their staff, like. There's no high-handedness or uppity behaviour from them. I couldn't ask for better employers. Ask any of the staff and they'll tell you the same."

"Thank you."

Mr Anderson was still far too ill to be interviewed, but from all the servants we spoke to we got the same reaction: John and Mary Anderson appeared to be universally loved by their employees. It was good to see, but also discouraging.

"I don't know," Alec said as we got back into the pony trap and headed for home. "Anyone could have got into that kitchen. I don't think we're any closer than when we started."

"Not just anyone," I said. "Surely not without being seen. They'd have to be quick to get in and out while Mrs Jenkins was in the larder. That must have been when they did it. And it was around the time that Doctor Carter excused himself. I'm afraid it all points right back to him."

Alec sighed. "It just seems like such an extreme thing to do. Could this really all be about the railway extension?"

"It looks that way."

"Sometimes I wonder who's running this investigation." He laughed and nudged me in a friendly way. Our eyes locked and he held my gaze for just a little too long. I was unsure if the churning in my stomach was because I felt excited or sick. I looked away and took a deep breath, suddenly awkward. Maybe I should never have agreed to work so closely with Alec.

We drove the rest of the way mostly in silence, each busy with our own thoughts. My composure had been jolted by that sudden small incident, and I didn't know what to think. When we pulled up outside my cottage he helped me down, and I found myself enjoying the feel of his hand on my waist even despite my misgivings. My heart was thumping.

"Good night, Alec," I said. "I'll see you tomorrow."

"Good night, Jane," he said, smiling. "I'd like that. It brightens my day, seeing you." Then he leaned in and kissed me on the cheek. My heart lurched but I didn't push him away. He climbed back into the buggy and I stood at the gate and watched until he was out of sight.

CHAPTER 12

I t took me a long time to get to sleep that night. Although I was tired, I kept replaying the memory of Alec's kiss over and over in my mind. I still wasn't sure what to think about it. On the one hand, it was nice to be desired, and it had been a long time since a man had looked at me like that— really, since Jim and I first began courting, for the romance there soon wore off. But the thought of tying myself to another man filled me with a visceral terror that I wasn't sure I'd ever get over. Although the memories were slowly fading, I still sometimes had nightmares about my marriage. But Alec was a good man on the face of it, and I knew I shouldn't judge all men by Jim. But then I'd thought Jim was a good man at the start too. And yet, if Alec were to kiss me again I didn't think I'd push him away. In fact, it was rather enjoyable to lie there and contemplate it.

My sleep, when it eventually came, was fitful and broken, and when I woke the next morning I still had no idea what I was going to do about Alec. I shook my head as I rose and dressed, endeavouring to put the problem from my mind. I'd see him that day and see what came of it. Likely as not, I was giving the whole incident far more weight than it deserved. We'd just continue on as normal.

Despite my resolutions, however, I couldn't help blushing when I entered the police station and saw him standing by the window, watching the traffic on the street. Hearing me come in, he turned towards me, smiling. I may have been imagining it, but it seemed like there was more than just politeness in his eyes; dare I say it, even affection. I also noticed—not for the first time, I'll admit—how erect his bearing was, and how the rough police uniform failed to hide a well-muscled body. Then I caught myself, for those kinds of thoughts were what had got me into trouble with Jim in the first place. Women weren't meant to think such things, I knew—Ma would have told me it was a sin. And I was very familiar with the wages of sin.

"Good morning," Alec said jovially. "Did you sleep well?"

If only he knew. "Well enough," I said. "You?"

He shrugged. "Can't complain. But I kept waking in the middle of the night thinking about the case."

"I'm still sure it's to do with the railway."

"You keep saying that, but I can't help feeling that we're missing something."

"What about the ghost train?"

"What about it?"

"Maybe that's the missing link."

He sighed, turning away from the window and coming over to me. I discreetly wiped my palms on my skirt; they'd grown unaccountably damp.

Alec took me gently by the shoulders and looked into my eyes. His own were a clear blue, like the summer sky. I was afraid to hold his gaze and afraid to look away.

"Jane," he said, his voice kind, "are you really sure about the ghost train? It's just that you're the only one to have seen it recently. Are you sure you couldn't have been mistaken?"

Whatever frisson there was between us shattered. I stepped back, forcing him to drop his hands from my shoulders. "Are you calling me a liar?"

"No, of course not. I'm just saying that sometimes we hear stories and our minds start to think they're real. And nobody thinks straight in the middle of the night." Without knowing it, he was echoing Annie Graham. I'd expected more from him.

"You don't believe me! You of all people!"

"Now Jane, come on..."

"Other people have seen it too, you know!"

He snorted derisively. "Polly Cruickshank. Hardly the most reliable witness. She's that gormless, she'd believe anything anybody told her."

"So you *do* think I'm lying!"

"I didn't say that. I'm just concerned about you. That note still bothers me. On the face of it, it seems to be obviously referring to John Anderson, but I'm just worried there's something I'm not seeing."

"There *is*—the ghost train!"

"Rubbish. Only madmen see ghosts."

"So now I'm deranged?"

He groaned in exasperation. "You *know* that's not what I meant. Why must you wilfully misunderstand everything I say?"

"You just don't want to have to take on Peter Maloney," I spat. "You're afraid that there's some truth to what I'm telling you and that you may actually have to show some moral fortitude where he's concerned."

"That's not fair, Jane."

"Tell me I'm wrong. Everything in the investigation points to him and yet you won't act unless I push you."

"I'm the policeman here—you shouldn't be pushing me to do anything. I'm in charge. I make the decisions!"

"I've heard that before." And I knew how it ended for women like me. I was stupid to think he could be different. "Fine! Do it your own way, Constable." I turned and marched out the door, ignoring his calls for me to come back. It was all I could do to hold back my tears, and not just because of his words. Alec was my only ally in this town, the only person I felt I could really trust. I'd assumed that he'd believe me, and it stung to realise how misplaced my confidence had been. I trudged up the main street, feeling despondent. How could the day have changed so fast? I just wanted to go home, wherever that was.

"Jane! Jane, wait!" I turned to see Edith Carter hailing me from outside the tea shop. Grace, Esme and Jessie were with her, of course. I sighed, pasting on a smile, because they were the last people I wanted to see right now. And why should they even want to talk to me after the way they'd treated me the other night?

"Ladies," I said as I approached, nodding to each of them.

"Mary asked us to pass on a gift," Grace said, holding out a jar of jam. "To say thank you for coming to dinner the other night, and welcome."

"That's very kind of her," I said, and I meant it. She was quite a woman, to be thinking of others at such a difficult time in her own life. "Please give her my thanks."

"Of course." There was an awkward silence, and I decided to put them out of their misery. They were clearly going to the tea shop and, just as clearly, none of them wanted the obligation of inviting me.

"I'm afraid I must go," I said. "I have to prepare for the afternoon train." It was a lie, of course—the train wasn't due until the evening, and there was no preparation to be done—but it did its job.

"Certainly. Don't let us keep you."

"Thank you for the jam."

All in all, it was a remarkably civil conversation, and I couldn't help being suspicious. But I didn't have the energy to mull it over; despite a slight lifting of my spirits at Mary's kindness, the pall of misery descended again as I walked out of town. It would take some time before I could fully forgive Alec for betraying my trust, if I ever could.

By the time I got home, I had little desire to do anything. I cut myself a couple of slices of bread, then opened Mary's jam. Strawberry—my favourite—and quite an indulgence, as I hadn't had the chance to make any myself. I ate the bread and jam, then tidied the kitchen and did some other chores, for the housework never stopped.

I was sweeping the verandah when I was overcome by a sharp pain in my stomach, as if I was being stabbed with a thousand needles. I doubled over, my broom clattering unheeded to the floor. The wave of pain passed, and I gasped with relief, only to be bowled over by another, worse one a few seconds later. Suddenly I knew I was going to be sick, and I leaned over the verandah railing just in time to heave my meagre lunch into the garden.

I staggered inside, the pain coming in increasingly close waves that left me groaning and gasping for breath. I lurched down the hallway to the telephone, one hand against the wall to keep myself upright. We weren't meant to use the telephone to make outside calls, but this was an emergency. "Doctor Carter's office," I gasped to the operator. "Quickly!"

Thankfully, Edith answered after only two rings. "It's Jane Adams," I told her, groaning as another wave of pain enveloped me. "I need help!"

"Where are you?"

"At home!"

"The doctor will be there as soon as he can."

"Please hurry! I think I'm dying!" As I went to hang up I was hit with the worst wave yet. I stumbled, clutching my stomach, the telephone receiver tumbling from my grasp. I crashed to the floor and the world went dark.

I woke through a thick fog, dimly recognising that I was in my own bed.

"Mrs Adams," Dr Carter said, "This is important. What did you eat?"

"Bread," I mumbled. "Jam." Then the fog claimed me again and I sank back into sleep.

When I woke again my head was clearer. There was still a dull ache in my stomach, and I felt weak and exhausted, but the stabbing pain had gone. Edith Carter, of all people, was sitting by the bed, acting as a kind of nurse, I supposed. My brain felt sluggish and slow, but I dimly noticed that the sheets were pink, not the white ones I normally used.

"Hello, Jane," she said. "How are you feeling?"

"The sheets are different," I said.

"We had to change them," she said. "You...evacuated yourself."

"Oh." I wanted to die of shame.

"It's all right," she said. "It was only the doctor and I here, and we've seen it all before, believe me."

"Oh," I said again. This was a side to Edith that I'd never seen. "What happened?"

Edith's eyes darkened. "The doctor thinks you were poisoned. You displayed exactly the same symptoms as John Anderson."

"What?" My brain felt sluggish.

"It seems to have been the jam." She shook her head, then turned at the sound of the front door opening. "That'll be the doctor coming back," she said. "I'll go and tell him you're awake."

But when she returned it wasn't Dr Carter who accompanied her, but Alec.

"Please don't ask too many questions, Constable," Edith said. "She's still very fragile." He nodded, staring at me with shock written all over his face. I must have looked worse than I realised.

Edith picked up a basin and a soiled cloth. "I'll be back soon," she said pointedly, closing the door behind her.

"Jane!" Alec sat in the bedside chair Edith had vacated and took my hand. "Are you all right? I've been so worried. You've been unconscious for nearly two days."

"Oh." I seemed able to say little else at the moment.

"Doctor Carter told me he thinks you were poisoned, the same as John Anderson. Do you know who might do such a thing?"

I shook my head against the pillow, and to my horror, hot tears began trickling down my cheeks. "It could have been anyone," I mumbled. "They all hate me."

"I'm sure that's not true." Alec stroked my hair off my forehead, a surprisingly tender gesture. I took a deep breath and got ahold of myself.

"The ghost train," I said. "It has to be. I know you don't believe me, but there's nothing else. And that jam—Grace Maloney gave it to me. She said it was from Mary, but I don't know that for sure."

"We'll see," he said soothingly. "Sleep now." I closed my eyes obediently, less because I felt tired than because I knew he still thought I was imagining it all, and I couldn't bear to see it in his eyes. And then at some point I stopped pretending to sleep and actually did.

The poison left me weak and shaky, and I was in bed for nearly a week recovering. I had no visitors except Edith and Dr Carter, and of course Alec, with whom I discussed everything but the case. As my strength returned, I became more and more convinced that someone wanted me away from the ghost train—as if the incidents with Bertha and the snakes hadn't shown that already. But Alec remained sceptical, and our early attempts to discuss it only left me angry and upset. I knew I was going to have to show him proof before he'd believe a word I said.

In truth, I'd actually begun to second-guess myself. It had been quite a while since I last saw the ghost train, and Alec's doubts had infected me; I wondered if in fact I had imagined it all. Perhaps he was right; perhaps it was just a nightmare brought on by the stories I'd heard around town.

And then I saw it again.

It was the same as the previous time; I was woken by the sound of wheels rattling on rails, and when I ran along the verandah to the railway side of the house, there it was, glowing eerily in the moonlight. I didn't see the spectral driver this time, but the sight of the train itself was enough to leave me feeling both chilled and vindicated. I knew now that I hadn't imagined it, no matter what Alec said.

I returned to my bed and lay there thinking. There must be a way to find out more about the ghost train. It didn't run every night, or even all that frequently, so what was special about the nights it did run?

I didn't for a minute think that the ghost train, despite its name, was in any way supernatural. It was just too real, too noisy, too visceral. And ghosts didn't nail dead chooks to your door or leave boxes of live snakes lying around. So there must be someone real involved. But who? And why? Why did it only run every now and again?

The answer came to me just as I was beginning to drift off to sleep. Perhaps it was a collection of people who were only periodically in the same place at the same time. I'd been so caught up with Peter Maloney, and maybe he *did* have something to do with it, but I couldn't see the grand squatter getting his hands dirty shovelling coal. Really, who better to run a ghost train than railway men? And who better to oversee their operations than my own boss, George Bailey? After all, he was the one who'd warned me about it in the first place—perhaps because he knew I'd start to wonder about an unscheduled train.

The more I thought about it, the more I was sure I was right. The ghost train ran when the railway conspirators were all rostered on at Tungold; now I just had to prove it. I had to see that roster.

CHAPTER 13

Far from being disabused of my midnight idea, when I woke the next morning I was more certain than ever that I'd hit on the truth. I was sitting on the verandah with a cup of tea, thinking it all over, when I saw Alec approaching on horseback. Although I'd been up and about for a few days, I hadn't yet felt strong enough to walk into town to see him, and he'd been calling on me every day. Even so, despite his solicitude, I decided to keep my theory to myself. I just knew he'd scoff at it or tell me I was crazy and, given that even seeing the roster might involve some breaking and entering, I figured it would be best if he knew nothing about it.

As it happened, the subject didn't even come up. When he tied his horse to the fence, I noticed that there was a bedroll and a large canvas bag slung behind the saddle.

"You going somewhere?" I asked as he joined me on the verandah.

"Just got the orders this morning," he said, sitting down. "They're having some trouble with bushrangers on the main road out west and they telegraphed to request me to join a party." He looked ecstatic at the thought; this was clearly the change he'd been waiting for.

"I take it you're happy about that?"

"Never happier than when I'm hunting crooks."

"How long will you be gone?"

"A few days; a week at most."

"What about the investigation?"

"Well, I couldn't very well refuse to go without telling them why, and to be honest, we've hit a bit of a dead end anyway. Both Mary Anderson and Grace Maloney—and their husbands, of course—swear they know nothing about the poison or why you might be targeted. I can't help thinking that a few days away might do me good. Hopefully it'll all be a bit clearer when I come back."

As long as no one gets murdered in the meantime, I thought, but I didn't say it. There was really no point. If someone really wanted to get me, then Alec was too far away to stop them even when he was in town, what with me being out here on my own.

"Maybe I'll have figured it all out by the time you return," I joked.

"Maybe you will have," he said with an indulgent smile, the kind you'd give a child.

After he left I sat a little longer, thinking. Really, his absence was perfect timing; it gave me the chance to see what I could find at the station. Of course, I wasn't naive enough to think that Mr Bailey would just show me the roster, especially if my theory was right. I was going to have to come up with another way.

I decided that I needed to visit the station first on some innocuous pretext, just to see what I was up against. The roster would be in Mr Bailey's office, but I couldn't remember where he kept the key. Right after the evening train arrived would be best; there'd be enough bustle around that my presence shouldn't seem too unusual.

Once I'd made my decision there was really nothing to do but wait, and the day crawled by with excruciating slowness. Eventually the telephone rang and I went and did my job, holding onto my hat as the train blew by. Once I'd reopened the gates I walked the short distance to the station.

It wasn't as busy as I'd hoped, and Mr Bailey spotted me immediately.

"Mrs Adams," he said. "What brings you here?" He snuffled into his moustache. "No problems, I hope?"

"No, sir, not at all. I...just wanted to check if there was going to be a new timetable issued soon. I want to make sure I'm fully aware of all the trains' movements." I was making it up as I went along, and could only hope it sounded plausible.

"That's very conscientious of you," Mr Bailey said, but his eyes narrowed slightly and I wondered if he knew what I was thinking. Thankfully, I was saved by one of the train lads calling for him down the other end of the platform. He excused himself and bustled off, giving me the chance to have a quick look around.

As I remembered, the door to Mr Bailey's office was stout wood with a sturdy brass lock. I'd seen he was wearing the key on his belt, so my chances of entering that way were practically non-existent. But what I'd failed to properly notice before was the window; it was small but not tiny, and I could probably squeeze through it, for I was quite sprightly and not large. It latched from the inside, but it was open tonight, what with the evening being so warm, and it was the work of a moment to twist the latch so that it wouldn't close effectively. I doubted Mr Bailey would even notice.

I was snapped back to my surroundings by the crunch of wheels on the platform. I turned around slowly, doing my best to look nonchalant, and breathed a sigh of relief when I saw that it was only Stanley Cruickshank with his trolley. I briefly glimpsed a fair-haired young woman behind him.

"Evening, Mrs Adams," Stanley said, tipping his cap. "Lucky you're here. Got a visitor for you, just arrived on the train."

He stepped aside and I got a proper view of the young woman. I reeled in shock, for it was my little sister, Lottie.

"I...thank you, Stanley," I spluttered. My words seemed to have deserted me. He had Lottie's trunk on his trolley—she'd brought a trunk, so she must be intending to stay for some time.

"Want me to take this to your place?"

"Ah...yes, thank you." I hugged Lottie, rather absently, then pulled away and looked at her properly, asking her with my eyes what was going on. *Later*, her gaze said. *When we're alone.*

Stanley prattled on as we walk back to my cottage, but I didn't hear a word of it. Lottie said nothing, and I was stunned into silence, which was almost unheard of.

"Where do you want it?" he asked as we reached the front door, referring to the trunk. It took me back to my own arrival in Tungold, not so very long ago, although it felt like years.

"In the bedroom." I gave the same answer as I gave then, for my cottage had only one bedroom, so we'd have to share. But what was she even doing here?

I was at least thinking clearly enough to find a coin for a tip, and Stanley seemed satisfied. He tipped his hat again and then left, whistling as he made his way back to the station. Lottie was still on the verandah. I went to her and embraced her properly this time, feeling suddenly as if I was about to cry.

"What brings you here?" I asked. She was the only one of my family to have stayed in touch through all the business with Jim, but I hadn't heard from her for some weeks. She would normally have let me know she was coming—she was too well-mannered to just turn up.

"I just wanted to see you. I missed you." There was clearly far more to the story than this, but I was going to have to coax it out of her.

"Well, I missed you too. It's wonderful to see you. Come inside. You must be exhausted after your journey." I was babbling a little, but mostly because I didn't know what to say. I watched her as she walked ahead of me, wondering. There was something slightly different about her, in the way she moved or the colour of her skin. I couldn't put my finger on it yet, although I had my suspicions—call it intuition. But we could talk about that later.

"Here, sit down," I said, ushering her into the kitchen. It wasn't a formal reception, but she was my sister. "Let me help you with your hat." I removed the pins for her and she rid herself of the hat gratefully, rubbing her head. It was just like old times.

"Tea?" I asked, setting the kettle on the hob.

"Thank you."

"It's so good to see you. You're looking well."

"Thanks. So are you. You seem much more relaxed. I suppose it's the country life."

I laughed at this. "I wouldn't say that. You'd be amazed at what goes on in a town like this."

"Go on then, tell me." She smiled that winsome, beautiful smile that I remembered. Lottie could always make the lads fall at her feet without even trying. Although I was dark and she was fair, with our green eyes and rosy cheeks we were very alike in looks—so much so that people often mistook us for twins, even though I was four years older and we had a brother in between. But the difference, as Ma had never tired of telling me, was that Lottie had the sweet personality to match her Irish Rose appearance, whereas I was mostly thorns.

"Just a moment," I said, catching sight of the clock and dashing out to close the level crossing gates just before the train thundered through on its way back to Goulburn. When I returned, I launched into an explanation of everything that had taken place since I arrived in Tungold, because I knew my sister well enough to realise that she didn't want to talk about whatever it was that had brought her here. She'd tell me in her own good time, and in the meantime, I had enough of a story to keep us occupied all night.

She laughed when I describe Grace Maloney and her cronies, but was startled when I told her of Brian's presence.

"Brian Mathieson? Isn't he that man that Jim worked for?"

"That's right."

"You had some trouble with him, didn't you?"

"We came to an...understanding."

"So what on earth was he doing here?"

"He said he was here to look at extending the railway line, but to be honest I'm not really sure. It doesn't matter much now anyway—he's dead."

"Dead!"

"Murdered."

"Surely not!" She was properly horrified, and I confess part of me was happy at disabusing her ideas of Tungold as a quiet little country town where nothing exciting happened. Plus I was keen to tell her about my part in the investigation.

"So you've got no idea who did it?" she asked some time later, after we'd chewed over all the facts of the case, including John Anderson's poisoning and my own, which shocked her deeply. "I wouldn't have thought there'd be too many people to choose from here."

"Well, they all seem to have alibis," I said. I was very proud to have learned the word 'alibi', and liked showing it off.

"Never mind," she said reassuringly. "I'm sure you'll crack the case eventually."

"Well, technically it's not my case; it's Alec's."

"Ah yes, Alec," she said, shooting me a sly grin. "Tell me more about him."

"There's nothing to tell," I said, even as I could feel my cheeks getting hot.

"Is there a Mrs Alec?"

"No."

"Well then."

"I'm not after a man, you know that. After Jim, I'm not sure I could face another one. You know what they're like."

Lottie's face clouded, and I wondered if I'd touched a nerve. She shouldn't know, not like that. I narrowed my eyes, watching her reaction, but there was pain in her gaze and I decided to move on.

"But yes, I confess I do like him," I said. "He's just a friend, though." The memory of his kiss rose unbidden, but I damped it down. I still wasn't sure if I desired or resented Alec. "And a sort of colleague, I suppose. Now, how about some dinner? I know it's late, but it's no trouble to make you something."

"Oh, I'm not very hungry, thanks."

"But you've been travelling for hours—you must be starving."

"I actually feel a bit unwell."

I started at this. "Should I fetch the doctor?"

"No, no, it's nothing. It'll pass. I might just go to bed, I think."

"Of course. You'll have to share with me; there's only one bed in the house."

"That's fine."

I showed her to the room and, once she was changed for bed, tucked her in like I used to when we were children. I still couldn't help mothering Lottie, no matter that she was a grown woman now herself. But she had always seemed so innocent; she was the kind of person one just felt the urge to protect.

"Call me if you need anything," I said. "I hope you feel better in the morning."

"I'm sure I will. Thank you, Jane." There was a degree of gratitude in her voice that seemed to outweigh anything I'd actually done for her, and again I wondered about the purpose of her visit. I poured myself another cup of tea and sat at the table, wondering as I drank it about this strange change in my fortunes. I also wondered about Ma and Da, and whether they even knew Lottie was here. She hadn't spoken about them at all—quite unusually for her—but she lived with them, so surely they must have known. Unless something else was going on that I had no idea about.

I finished my tea and washed the cup, then decided to go to bed. Lottie was breathing deeply and steadily as I climbed in beside her, but, sensing the movement, she rolled over and put her arm around me. It had been such a long time since I'd been held with any affection that I couldn't help sobbing quietly into my pillow as I drifted into a deep, dreamless sleep.

My mind must have been working even as I slept, for I woke with a strange idea that I couldn't seem to shake. I let Lottie sleep while I stoked the fire and pumped water, but as I was cooking breakfast she wandered into the kitchen in her nightclothes, perhaps awoken by the enticing smell of frying bacon.

"You're just in time," I said, handing her a plate. "What would you like?"

"Oh, nothing," she said. "I'm still feeling a bit ill."

I looked at her keenly and decided to confront the matter head-on. Subtlety had never been my strong suit.

"How far along are you?"

She looked startled at this; perhaps she'd thought I wouldn't be able to guess. But she didn't deny it.

"Not very far. About three months, I think."

"Oh, Lottie." I took her in my arms as she started to cry, stroking her hair as if she were a child. Part of me wanted to chastise her; after everything that had happened to me, how could she go and do such a thing? Surely she'd known what the consequences would be?

I didn't say anything, but she seemed to sense my disapproval, or perhaps she just knew me too well. "It's not what you think, Jane."

"Will there be a wedding?" When it had happened to me, our parents had insisted on one, nice and quick, before I'd had time to show.

She shook her head, which surprised me. "But Ma and Da have thrown you out?" I pressed. I needed to know.

She nodded, and I felt my heart sink. "Because they thought I wouldn't tell them who the father is."

"Why not? Are you afraid they'd force you to marry him?" Knowing our parents, it was a reasonable fear.

"I *did* tell them, but they wouldn't believe me."

"What do you mean?"

"I told them the truth, but Ma called me a liar and a whore and told me to get out." I sighed, for our mother had called me similar things when I'd first confessed to my mistake. She hadn't thrown me out of the house, but in the two weeks between the revelation and the hastily organised wedding, she hadn't spoken a word to me; this had continued after my marriage and even after Jim's death. I'd brought the ultimate shame on the family; to have both daughters fall pregnant out of wedlock would shatter her beyond all reason.

"Who is it, Lottie? I promise I'll believe you."

"It's Uncle Bob."

Her words hit me like a physical blow, and I thought I was going to be sick. I ushered Lottie to a chair and pressed my hands to my mouth, trying to stop them shaking. Uncle Bob was our father's best friend, another Irishman. They'd met on the transport ship and stayed in touch after they won their freedom. But where Da went straight, Uncle Bob was always into shady dealings. And he had an eye for young girls. Unbidden, I remembered how, when I was only fifteen, he'd bailed me up against the shed wall. But I'd already begun to run with a pretty tough crowd by then, so he got a knee to the groin for his trouble and a warning that he'd better keep his hands to himself in future if he wanted to retain the use of them. He could tell that I meant it too. I never had any trouble with him after that, but I'd also never told anyone what had happened. Ma and Da wouldn't have believed me, and I'd been too caught up in my own affairs to even think about Lottie. But a sweet young thing like her, who was kind to everyone and a bit too innocent for her own good, would have been the perfect prey. At that moment I vowed he would get his comeuppance, even if it took me the rest of my life to make it happen.

"How many times?" I asked, although I wasn't sure I wanted to know the answer.

"Three," she sobbed. "When he was visiting from Sydney."

"It's all right," I whispered, holding her. "We'll figure it out. You can stay here and it's all going to be all right." I hoped I wasn't promising too much.

"Thank you," she whispered. "I didn't have anywhere else to go."

Now that the issue was out in the open, Lottie seemed relieved. But she was still tired and sick, so I sent her back to bed with a cup of strong ginger tea and a bucket. I ate my breakfast—although I could hardly taste it—and took my own cup of tea to the rocking chair on the verandah. I liked to think that if our parents could only see the truth, they'd take her back, but I was in sad agreement with my sister that they were unlikely to believe her, especially when she'd already tried to be honest with them. And they certainly wouldn't believe me; our relationship was broken beyond repair. I didn't hate my parents, despite everything, but I no longer trusted them to do the right thing. I'd learned a long time ago that I had to look after myself, and now I was the only one left to look after Lottie too.

I started doing sums in my head, growing increasingly worried. My salary was enough for me to live on in relative comfort, but could it also support Lottie and a baby? Lottie would probably have to get a job too, but who would employ a young woman tainted by such scandal? Annie Graham might be prevailed upon; even a kitchen-maid position would be better than nothing. I knew I was racing ahead, but I couldn't help it. Planning stopped me from thinking too much about Uncle Bob and what my poor sister must have gone through. I swore to myself that I would never let anyone hurt her again.

I spent the rest of the morning pottering around in the garden, fretting. I never ceased to be amazed how quickly life could change; how a single action could have consequences that reverberated long after the deed itself was over and done.

The next few days were a kind of limbo: the stress of the journey seemed to have taken its toll on Lottie, and she spent much of the time in bed. When she had the strength to get up, we sat in the garden under the shade of the trees, or on the verandah, discussing nothing of consequence, just like old times. Presently we began reminiscing about our childhoods, about running wild with our brothers, back when we thought we could do and be anything we wanted. We hadn't realised then how many paths would be closed to us just by virtue of our sex. It was bittersweet; there was much laughter, but more than once I felt a lump in my throat, thinking of how things had turned out. But we were here now and we had to make the best of it.

Despite my worry for her, I was the happiest I'd been since arriving in Tungold—I hadn't quite realised how much I'd been missing such companionship. I felt a lightness that I hadn't felt for a long time, and a deep love and gratitude for my sister. I honestly didn't know what I'd do without her. It would be hard, the two of us and the baby, but at that moment I felt that we could conquer anything, as long as we were together.

On the third morning after Lottie's arrival, I woke to find the other side of the bed empty. For a moment I was struck by a pang of panic, but then I heard noises coming from the kitchen. On entering, I was surprised but happy to find her pottering around making breakfast.

"Feeling better?" I asked.

"Much better, thanks. Here, have something to eat." She handed me a plate and I accepted it gratefully.

"What would you like to do today?" I asked, sitting down at the table.

"I was actually thinking about walking into town. I could use the fresh air and exercise. What do you think?"

"Are you sure?" I asked. "The Tungold folk are a nosey lot—they'll ask plenty of questions, I assure you."

"That's all right," she said. "We can just tell them the truth, or part of it at least. I'm your sister from Goulburn, and I've come to stay with you for a while, for a change of scene. I'm not showing yet, so I doubt any of them will notice. And if they do, we can always say I'm married."

"You're not wearing a ring."

She shrugged. "I'll keep my gloves on."

"Here," I said, sliding my own wedding band off and handing it to her. "Wear this. Just in case."

She stared at me, and I realised it must seem like an odd gesture. "Are you sure?"

"Of course. It doesn't mean anything to me anymore. I don't even know why I still wear it."

"Won't people talk if they see you without it?"

"I'm a widow—what does it matter? They've already paired me off with Alec in their minds anyway."

"Have they, now? And why would they do that?"

"Probably because we're both new to town and unmarried, and they love a good gossip."

"No other reason?"

"It's not like that."

She smiled, and I realised I'd forgotten what it was like to have someone around who knew me so well. Normally I could hide my feelings quite effectively, but not from Lottie. "But you want it to be, don't you?" she said, teasingly.

"I honestly don't know," I said, and it was the truth. "I don't necessarily want to go through life as an ageing widow, but having a man around often leads to more trouble than satisfaction, in my experience."

"Not all men are like Jim, you know." She said this with a fondness in her eyes, which, after everything that had happened, was surprising.

"You had a sweetheart back in Goulburn," I said, slightly shocked, as realisation dawned. I still thought of Lottie as my baby sister, far too young for sweethearts.

She nodded. "Not any more, though," she said, her lip trembling. "Not after all this. Probably never again." She placed the pan on the hob with a clatter, wiping her eyes.

"There, there," I said, getting up and putting my arms around her. Maybe we should go into town after all, if only to distract her. "There now, how about that walk?"

She nodded again, blowing her nose on her handkerchief. "I'm fine, really," she said. "I just haven't been myself lately."

"It will be all right, I promise," I said as we readied ourselves to go out. "You're here now, and I won't let anything happen to you."

But as we set off down the bright sunshiny road, I reflected on those words and wondered. Was that a promise I'd be able to keep, or had I just told Lottie the biggest lie of all?

CHAPTER 14

I t was a pleasant walk into town, for the day's heat hadn't yet peaked. Lottie gazed around her as we walked, taking everything in, and I remembered my own first day in Tungold, when it was all new. It wasn't so very long ago, but it felt like years. I wondered if I could pass for a local yet. I suspected Grace Maloney might have something to say about that.

Truth be told, I was walking along in dread of encountering Grace and the other ladies. I worried that they'd be able to see through Lottie's facade. I still wasn't sure where I fitted into this town, and the thought of being cast out again was difficult to bear. But my loyalty of course lay with my sister, and they were going to find out eventually. We'd just have to concoct some sort of plausible story before they did. I let my mind drift, starting to invent a husband for Lottie, who would have to meet with some sort of misfortune just as she began to show. It would make sense for her to come and live with her widowed sister in such a state, and who would be able to say it was untrue? I wished she'd taken up my offer of the wedding band, but when we left it had still been sitting on the table, and I hadn't wanted to press the issue.

"What are you thinking about?" Lottie asked as we ambled along. My pensiveness must have shown on my face.

"Oh, nothing much." I couldn't tell her the truth. I didn't want her to know how worried I was about her.

"What a pretty little town," she said, as the main street came into view. That hadn't been my first impression of Tungold, but Lottie had always had a knack for seeing the best in things. Even though we were sisters, we really couldn't have been more different in terms of personality, but that difference was complementary. She needed me to look out for her, and I needed her to remind me of the beauty in life. I couldn't have survived those years with Jim without her, especially after Ma and Da cut me off.

"It's not too bad," I said. "The locals are a funny lot, but they'll warm to you eventually." Everyone liked Lottie; it was impossible not to. I was sure she'd have an easier time settling into Tungold than I had.

It was market day, and a lot of the farmers from roundabout had brought their produce into town and set up stalls in the main street. The place was bustling. I'd completely forgotten that it would be when she'd suggested we walk into town. Annie Graham was the first person we ran into, although she nearly didn't see us as she was deep in conversation with Matthew Maloney, of all people. When I called her name she looked up, startled, as if she'd been caught doing something she oughtn't.

"Mrs Graham, this is my sister Lottie," I said. "She's come to stay with me for a while."

"Pleasure," Annie said, and as she looked into Lottie's face, I could tell she meant it. Lottie had a wholesome, open sweetness about her that was undeniably attractive. She drew people to her without even realising she was doing it.

We continued on through the market, and I bought one or two things, although I was more conscious than ever about watching my pennies. But when I saw Lottie eyeing a small bar of chocolate in the grocer's window, I ducked in surreptitiously and bought it for her anyway, despite its cost. I couldn't help wanting to spoil her, and she'd had little enough joy in her life of late that this small thing was the least I could do. When I gave it to her, she grinned and hugged me—you'd have thought I'd given her the moon. I realised again just how much I'd missed her.

It was probably inevitable that we'd run into Grace and the others, as market day was a major event on the Tungold social calendar, so I wasn't that surprised when we did. I introduced Lottie to them and stood back to gauge their reactions. I still remembered how unfriendly they'd been to me when I first came to town.

"It's a pleasure to meet you, dear," Grace said, a trifle patronisingly but apparently sincerely. "Darling Jane has certainly shaken things up in this town, what with playing policewoman and all." She tittered, and the others followed suit as if she'd made some great joke. I bit my tongue at *darling Jane*.

I needn't have worried about how the ladies would accept Lottie; they took to her immediately, much as one might to a puppy or kitten. There was something about Lottie that invited protection. Even Esme Johnson seemed flattered when Lottie smiled in her direction. I had no idea how my sister did it, and all completely unconsciously. She wasn't trying to charm or influence anyone; there was just something about her character that bowled people over. It was a gift I wished I had. I could manipulate folk well enough, but I couldn't attract them the way Lottie did.

Interestingly enough, it was Edith Carter who didn't seem completely convinced. There was something about the way she looked at Lottie that made me think she wasn't entirely sold on our story. It didn't help that Lottie was starting to look decidedly green again, and I began to wonder if coming into town had been such a good idea. From Edith's time as my nurse I knew that she was more perceptive than many gave her credit for, and she didn't miss this.

"Are you quite well, dear?" she asked Lottie softly, just loud enough for me to hear. Lottie's eyes widened in alarm, but she quickly covered it with a smile.

"Yes, quite, thank you," she said, although it was clear she was fighting a wave of nausea. I bit my lip in consternation, hoping she wouldn't be sick, but Edith said nothing further.

We joined the ladies on their perambulation through the market, and the others were clearly enjoying turning various male heads with their finery. Lottie was at the front of the group with Grace, who seemed to have made her a personal pet. Jessie and Esme were slightly behind, and I'd fallen further behind them. I was lost in my thoughts, and jumped slightly when Edith appeared beside me.

"Is your sister in trouble?" she asked quietly, taking me completely by surprise.

"What?" I asked, trying not to let the shock show on my face. "No, of course not. She's just visiting." I quickly glanced ahead at Lottie. She definitely wasn't showing; apart from the sickness, there was no obvious indication.

Edith looked contrite. "I don't mean to pry," she said, "but I've known a lot of girls in that particular sort of trouble over the years, and I've got very good at noticing the little signs. It's to do with being a doctor's wife, plus I've birthed five myself. I know what it's like to go about your daily business trying not to show how rotten you feel. How far along is she?"

I gave up. "About three months."

"And no husband?"

I shook my head, and she took my elbow, leading me out of the main market traffic to where we were less likely to be overheard. Lottie and the other ladies walked on, oblivious.

"The thing is," she continued, "my husband can help. He often assists women in the district who are in difficulties, if you know what I mean."

I raised my eyebrows, because I *did* know what she meant. "He's breaking the law."

She shrugged. "Technically, maybe. But this is a poor region, and many of these women already have too many mouths to feed. How do you tell a desperate mother of twelve that she'll just have to find room for one more? Or an unmarried young girl that her life will be ruined because of one silly mistake?"

"I don't know."

"Just...think about it. I'm not going to ask for any details, but if you could just let your sister know. You know where to find us if you need us."

I nodded again, not sure what to say. We rejoined the crowd and caught up to the ladies, and nothing more was said about it, but I wondered. I'd have to mention it to Lottie, and then it would be up to her to make a decision. This was one thing I couldn't do for her.

I was wandering along in a bit of a daze, and I was so distracted that I didn't notice Alec until I literally almost ran into him.

"You're back!" I exclaimed without thinking.

"Nice to see you too," he said with a grin. "May I join you?"

"Of course."

He offered me his arm and I took it—it seemed like the polite thing to do.

"Did you catch any bushrangers?" I asked.

"As a matter of fact, we did. Got Captain Starlight himself."

"Really? That's quite a coup for you." I glanced down towards the police station, as if I'd see the infamous man himself being hauled in for his crimes. "Where have you put him? In the cells here?"

"Not exactly. He's dead."

"Dead?" I frowned. "Did you kill him?"

He shrugged in assent. "He was guilty."

"I don't doubt it, but still..." A thought occurred to me. "Wasn't he the one who shot you?"

"Yes."

"So it was revenge." I hadn't thought he could be so ruthless.

"No, it was justice. We could have taken him in for trial, but he would have just been hanged anyway. The others agreed, and they were more than happy to look the other way."

"So you didn't just kill him, you *executed* him?" I was rather horrified that Alec could be capable of such a thing.

"Tell me honestly, Jane—would you have done any different?"

I bit my lip, saying nothing for a long moment. But then I knew I had to concede. "No. I wouldn't have."

"Well, then." But even so, I couldn't help picturing the bushranger on his knees in the dirt, hands tied behind his back, with Alec holding a pistol to his head. I wondered how well I really knew this man.

"I don't suppose you've cracked the case while I've been gone?" he asked jokingly, clearly trying to bring some levity to the situation.

"Well, I still think Peter Maloney did it," I said distractedly. "Or at least, he and some co-conspirators."

"Facts, Jane, facts."

"All right, you want facts? Mr Maloney and Doctor Carter are at the heart of this business with the railway. They both staunchly oppose it, for reasons that I don't quite understand. Then Brian comes to town, crowing about how he's looking into the viability of an extension. For some reason, this threatens the squatter's plans. And Brian is already onto a bigger conspiracy to remove John Anderson, the other proponent of the extension, from the equation. So Peter Maloney takes the necessary action and deals with Brian. And then it's just a matter of carrying out their plans for Mr Anderson. So the doctor goes to dinner, taking some drugs from his surgery, and slips out during the meal and puts them in Mr Anderson's food. But the dose isn't quite strong enough, and Mr Anderson lives. So now they're in a bit of a bind. I doubt they'll try again; it would be too obvious. But in the meantime, they also try to warn me off asking questions about the ghost train, which is somehow connected to all this too. And they've sent a pretty strong message that anyone who opposes their ideas for the railway will be dealt with."

"That's a fascinating story, but..."

"Neither of them will tell us where they were the night Brian died, and we know Doctor Carter had time to poison the food at the Andersons' party," I said. "It all fits perfectly. I don't know why you don't just arrest them."

"We'll need to talk to them again, certainly," Alec conceded. "I'll impress upon them the importance of us knowing their movements on both nights. You'll probably find they have alibis."

"Why are you so quick to defend them?"

He sighed. "You may not like Mr Maloney and Doctor Carter, but they've done a lot for this town. Towns like this need their pillars of society. If you remove them, things start to crumble."

"That's not a good enough reason to leave them free. Don't you believe in justice?"

"Of course I do. But I just don't want to be too hasty. We have to make sure we're not jumping to conclusions. If I get incontrovertible proof, then of course I'll arrest them. But first I want their alibis."

"I can see we're going to have to agree to disagree on this."

"Not at all—but you're new to police work, Jane. It doesn't always move as efficiently as you might like. There are processes we have to follow."

I baulked at the patronising tone in his voice and stared straight ahead. We'd clearly reached an impasse.

The other ladies had hung back, waiting for me, and now they noticed Alec.

"Good afternoon, ladies," he said, tipping his hat. He really did look very smart in his uniform, but I wasn't sure I was entirely comfortable with him anymore, now that I knew what he was capable of.

"Good afternoon, Constable Ward," Esme said, simpering. I hadn't realised she had designs on Alec, and I felt a flash of something that seemed suspiciously like jealousy. But then I saw her watching Grace's reaction out of the corner of her eye, and I wondered if something else was going on. It was almost like she was trying to prove to Grace that she was interested in Alec. But why? Damn these women and their infernal machinations.

Grace was already introducing Lottie to Alec, completely subsuming my prerogative as her sister. He nodded politely to her and she smiled sweetly back. I felt rather superfluous to the situation.

I tried to shake off the feelings of despondency, and smiled when Alec and the ladies looked my way. Eventually he tipped his hat again and took his leave, but as he passed he caught my arm. I stopped and the rest of the group moved on without me.

"May I call tonight?" he asked. I shook my head.

"Not tonight. Lottie needs to rest. She's been ill."

"May I at least walk you home? Please, Jane. I know we disagree sometimes, but I really do need your help on this case."

"We're not going home just yet. We have some shopping to do."

Alec seemed to know when he was beaten; he just nodded and walked away.

Lottie must have noticed my dejected air, for she managed to extract herself from the ladies' clutches and dropped back to take my arm.

"Are you all right?" she asked.

"Yes, of course. I'm just feeling the heat a little."

"Why don't we go and look at the shops? It'll be cooler out of the sun."

I smiled gratefully as she made our excuses to the ladies and led me across the road into the dimness of the haberdasher's. As it happened, I was glad she'd chosen this shop. It had been her birthday the previous month and I hadn't sent her a present, for the shawl I'd been knitting had taken longer to finish than I'd anticipated. Ever since she'd arrived I'd been thinking about making her a new dress, for all her frocks were going to need letting out anyhow, and I knew how infrequently she'd had new clothes at home. My better judgement reminded me of the cost, but I quashed it. I couldn't seem to help being extravagant where Lottie was concerned.

Inside the haberdasher's, I thumbed through their new stock of fabric. Lottie looked confused when I asked her to choose.

"What's this for?" she asked.

"A new dress," I said. "Choose what you like and I'll make it up for you. It's your birthday present, albeit somewhat belated."

"It's too much, Jane."

"Rubbish. Either you choose or I'll choose for you, and knowing the differences in our taste, I doubt you'll want that." She laughed and began perusing the material, running it through her fingers. Eventually she settled on a smart dark blue poplin, elegant but not over-fine. It suited her perfectly, with her rosy cheeks and fair hair. I paid for the material and we took our parcel, then I led Lottie towards the tea shop. She didn't protest as we settled down to tea and homemade scones with jam and fresh cream. The colour had returned to her cheeks, and she didn't turn away from the food.

"What a treat," she said with a smile, and my heart swelled with happiness.

"My pleasure," I said. Our table was by the window and it was very pleasant sitting there watching the world go by. We didn't make much conversation, because sometimes we both enjoyed just sitting in each other's company. It had always been that way.

"Who's that?" Lottie asked after some time, pointing out the window. "He looks pretty angry."

I followed her direction and saw none other than Peter Maloney, striding red-faced down the main street, gesturing furiously at someone out of our sight.

"That's Peter Maloney, the squatter from Queensgrace," I said. "Grace's husband."

"Does he make a habit of storming down the main street?"

"Not usually, but he's an odd one." I glanced at her conspiratorially. "Shall we go and see what the fuss is about?" She returned my grin, for Lottie wasn't above a little gossip now and then. It was what stopped her from being an insufferable prude.

We paid for our tea and left the shop, walking along the covered verandah in the same direction as Peter, pretending that we were going to visit one of the other stores. I kept glancing across to make sure we hadn't lost him. Standing on the porch of the baker's, which was next to the hotel, we found Esme Johnson. She was watching the proceedings with rapt concentration and barely noticed us.

"What's going on?" I asked her.

"Shh!" she hissed.

Soon the object of Peter Maloney's wrath became clear. "You mind your own business!" he bellowed at Annie Graham, who was still standing on the hotel verandah talking to Matthew Maloney. "You interfering old busybody!" Annie noticed him and looked up, startled. From my vantage point I could see a slow flush creeping up Matthew's cheeks.

"How dare you!" Peter continued, in full flight. "We had an agreement!"

"Would you like to come inside?" Annie asked. I was amazed by her calm.

"Inside your filthy establishment? No thank you! I'll say what I have to say right here!"

"You've never objected to my establishment when you've wanted a beer."

"Oh no," I whispered to Lottie, nudging her and indicating Grace Maloney, who was tearing up the street as fast as her dignity would allow. Someone must have alerted her to the commotion. She reached her husband just as he launched into another tirade.

"Peter!" she hissed, grabbing his arm. "Stop it! You're making a scene!" But the squatter shook her off as if she was little more than an annoying insect, and turned his attention to his son.

"You come down here right now!" he railed. "I never want you to speak to that woman again, do you hear?"

"But Dad..."

Peter Maloney bounded onto the verandah and grabbed Matthew by the ear. "Don't you 'but Dad' me! When I tell you to do something, you do it!" Annie inserted herself between them, and for one terrible moment, I feared Peter was going to strike her.

"I'm going to fetch Constable Ward," I said to Lottie and Esme, although the latter appeared not to hear me. "This is getting out of hand." I turned to hurry away, but as I did, I noticed a familiar figure coming up the street. A small crowd was growing outside the shops, watching from a safe distance; one of them must have told Alec already.

He reached the scene just in time to stop things getting worse. He deftly placed himself between the warring parties, giving Annie and Matthew room to back away, and caught Peter Maloney's raised arm.

"Now, sir, I think it's time to calm down," he said. "What exactly is the problem here?"

"That...*bitch* has been corrupting my boy!"

"Please mind your language, sir; there are ladies present. Now, why don't we go inside and see if we can get all this sorted out?"

"I'm not going in there with her!"

"Mr Maloney, we can either discuss the matter inside the hotel or at the police station. Your choice."

Peter Maloney seemed to deflate as we watched. I figured he must have realised that a discussion at the police station would involve being frogmarched by the constable back down the main street, and he wanted to save what little face he had left. Apart from the fight at the dance, it was the first time I'd really seen Alec in action, and I was impressed.

"After you, Mrs Maloney," he said, ushering Grace into the pub. Then he turned to us.

"Mrs Adams, Miss Johnson, Miss O'Donohue. Did you happen to see what occurred?"

"Some of it," I said.

"Then perhaps you'd better join us."

We did as he said, not least because I wanted to see how it would all turn out. This was the most exciting thing to happen in Tungold since John Anderson's poisoning.

CHAPTER 15

Alec directed us to the dining room and we all took our seats—Lottie, Esme and I back from the main offenders. Peter Maloney and Annie Graham were still glowering at each other across the table.

"Now," Alec said, "can someone shed some light on what's going on here?" Nobody spoke.

"Mrs Adams," Alec said, turning to me. "What did you see?"

"I saw Mr Maloney come running up Main Street looking very angry," I said. "He seemed to be upset that Mrs Graham was talking to his son."

"And why would that be, Mr Maloney?" Alec asked. Peter Maloney glared but said nothing.

"The only way we're leaving here is if we resolve this matter, or, alternatively, I charge you both with disturbing the peace and take you down to the station," Alec said. Esme covered her mouth with her hand in apparent shock. "So I'd say it's in everyone's interests to start talking."

"She knows she has to stay away from my boy," Peter muttered.

"And why is that?"

"We have an agreement."

"Mrs Graham, is this true?"

"Well...we did, a long time ago. But Matthew is a man now. He should be able to make his own choices."

"And why is that relevant?"

"He's my son!" Peter interjected again.

Annie muttered something.

"What was that, Mrs Graham?"

"I said, not by blood, he isn't."

Esme gasped again and I glanced across at her. She was looking at Grace Maloney, but the squatter's wife had bowed her head.

"What do you mean?"

"It's rubbish," Peter blustered. "Don't you believe a word of it, Matthew!"

Matthew Maloney, having unwillingly found himself at the centre of the storm, looked tired and careworn. "It's all right, Dad," he said. "I know all about it."

"*What?*"

"Would someone please explain from the beginning?" Alec asked.

"All right," Annie said with a sigh. "Many years ago, before I met my late husband, I was being courted by a young man. He was a shearer who'd come to work at Queensgrace. It was only after he left Tungold to take up work elsewhere that I realised I was in trouble—and he never came back. I couldn't afford to keep the baby, and I knew Grace and Peter had been trying to have children without success. So we came to an arrangement—they would raise the child as their own, and none of us would say any more about it.

"From the moment I handed my beautiful little boy over it was harder than I ever thought it could be. I hoped it would get easier as the years went on, but watching him grow into a fine young man only made me wish I'd known him better. I know we said we'd never tell him, but I just couldn't help myself..." Tears welled up in her eyes and spilled down her cheeks.

"How long have you known?" Alec asked Matthew.

"About six months," he said, and Grace looked up with a start. "I couldn't believe it at first, but then it started to make sense. So Annie and I have been meeting every now and again to talk. You're still my parents," he said, turning imploringly to Grace and Peter. "Nothing will ever change that. But I needed to know where I come from."

The Maloneys were silent as they took it all in, and I could see Alec putting the pieces together in his head. It seemed like Mrs Graham's secrecy had been explained.

"So, on the night that Brian Mathieson was killed, you were visiting Matthew?" he asked her. She nodded. "Brian found out and threatened to tell Peter and Grace if I didn't pay him off. I didn't have the cash, but he never paid a penny for his room or board here. That night, Matthew had told me that his parents were both going to be out, so I went down to Queensgrace. But not before I saw Peter here, going up to Brian's room."

"What time was this?"

"Around seven o'clock."

171

"Care to explain what you were doing there, Mr Maloney?" Alec asked.

"I told you before, Constable, I came to tell him to mind his own business. He kept insisting on poking his nose in where it wasn't wanted. But I didn't kill him, if that's what you're asking. He was alive and well when I left, sure as I'm sitting here talking to you."

Doesn't mean you didn't double back and kill him later, I thought. Alec clearly had the same idea, for he asked, "And where did you go after you left the hotel? Home?"

"Uh...I don't remember."

"Really? That's unfortunate."

Grace Maloney snorted in a most unladylike fashion. "Mrs Maloney?" Alec asked. "Have you got something to say?"

"Doesn't remember, my foot," she snapped, glaring at her husband. "You were with *her*." Peter Maloney blanched, the colour draining so quickly from his face that for a moment I feared he was going to faint. His mouth opened and closed like a fish's, but no sound came out.

"Oh yes," Grace continued. "You thought I didn't know? You stupid, arrogant man."

"Grace..." Esme began, but Mrs Maloney cut her off.

"How dare you!" she said, her voice icy. "All this time, pretending to be my friend, while all along you were...liaising...with my husband. You're nothing but a cheap whore who doesn't even have the dignity of being paid for her wares!"

Esme began to tremble uncontrollably, and I bit back a surge of glee at all these vile people getting their comeuppance. I'd known they weren't as perfect as they made out to be; nobody was.

"How did you know?" Peter murmured.

"I *saw* you," Grace said. "I'm not stupid, you know. It was so obvious when you started going out of an evening, so that night I told you I had a Ladies' Auxiliary meeting, then I got Timothy to take me into town and I followed you. You came here, and then you went to *her* house."

Alec turned to Peter. "You say you went to see Brian to tell him to mind his own business. What business was that, exactly?"

Peter sighed. "The bastard was trying to blackmail me too."

"Oh?"

"He knew Esme and I had been...seeing...each other. He saw us together one night, when we were saying goodbye. And then he threatened to tell Grace unless I did what he wanted. I tried to reason with him but he was tough. So I went to see Esme to tell her we had to end it. It was getting too risky to continue."

"Miss Johnson?"

"That's right," Esme sobbed. "Peter was with me from around half-past seven...all night."

"And you, Mrs Maloney," Alec said. "What did you do after you followed your husband to Miss Johnson's house? Did you go home?"

Grace sighed. "No. I came back here."

"To see Brian?"

She looked at him like he was crazy. "Of course not. Why would I want to see that odious man? I...no, it's too humiliating."

"What did you do?"

"She came and sat in my back bar and drowned her sorrows," Annie said, raising an eyebrow. "Polly served her while I was out. When I got home around midnight she was still there, singing like a sailor. Not the best look for the chairwoman of the Temperance League," she added snidely. *So much for the ban on serving women*, I thought.

Grace Maloney buried her face in her hands. "It was a terrible lapse in judgement," she said. "If it should ever get out...I don't know how I'd live it down."

"Anyway," Annie continued, "between us, Timothy and I got her back into the carriage so he could take her home. I imagine the maids put her to bed. She wouldn't have been in the best shape the next day." She smirked, and Grace started sobbing.

"Well now," Alec said, "I'm glad we've sorted everything out for the time being. But I think you all need to have a civilised conversation at another time, when everyone isn't quite so...emotional." They all nodded, chastened.

I'd been feeling increasingly uncomfortable, so I was glad when the party broke up shortly afterwards. I hadn't expected to be privy to so much private business. And, in truth, the only thing I could really think about was that our list of suspects had shortened considerably. It now looked unlikely that Peter Maloney had killed Brian, although he could still have been responsible for John Anderson's poisoning—and mine. It seemed like just as we appeared to get hold of a solid suspect they came up with an alibi. I sighed.

"Penny for your thoughts?" Alec said, coming over to where I was standing on the pub verandah, looking back towards town. Edith and Jessie had emerged from the crowd and commandeered Lottie, clearly wanting the inside story.

"I don't think they're worth that much."

We stood for a few minutes in a silence that grew increasingly uncomfortable, but I wasn't about to break it.

"Can we start again, Jane?" Alec asked eventually. "Whatever I've said to offend you, I'm sorry for it. And I really do need your help on this case."

"I'm not sure I can help you much more than I already have," I said coldly, but he looked so downcast that I relented. "Oh, all right. Would you do me the service of walking us home?"

"Of course. And thank you." We joined Lottie and the two ladies, but I noticed Lottie was starting to look pale, despite her smile, so as soon as I could I pulled her aside.

"Everything all right?"

"To be honest, I'm not feeling all that well," she said. "Do you think we could go home soon?"

"Of course."

We took our leave from Edith and Jessie, who fussed over Lottie like little sparrows. Eventually Alec assured them that he would see us safely home, and extracted us. I hated to admit it, but I was grateful, and Lottie gave a sigh of relief once we were finally on the road out of town.

"They can be a bit much, can't they?" Alec said with a smile.

"I'm sure they all mean well," she said. Lottie never said a bad word about anyone.

"They're a bunch of scurrilous old gossips," I said, for I was not like my sister.

"So how do you like Tungold?" Alec asked Lottie, deftly changing the subject.

"It's a pretty little town," she said. "I like it very well."

"Do you think you'll be staying long?"

Lottie glanced at me. "Probably some time."

"I'm sure your sister is glad to have you. It must get lonely in that cottage with only the ghost train for company, right, Jane?"

I frowned at him in warning but it was too late. Lottie was intrigued.

"What ghost train?"

"Jane hasn't told you? There's a ghost train that runs along here at night. They say it carries the souls of those bound for hell." He laughed, but Lottie's eyes widened, and I sighed. She'd always been one for fanciful stories—she'd believed that there were fairies at the bottom of our garden until she was twelve—and I hadn't been planning to tell her about the ghost train for fear that she'd be scared. Too late now. Bloody Alec.

"Gosh. Does it run every night? I didn't hear anything the last few nights."

"No," I said, "just now and again."

"Have you seen it, Jane?"

"Twice." Alec started at that, for I hadn't told him about the second time, but I wasn't going to go into it now.

"Was it terrifying?"

"It was eerie enough."

"I wonder if I'll see it?"

"I doubt it. Best to stay in bed. Oh, I forgot to tell you," I added, trying to change the subject, "Constable Ward is a keen gardener. He helped me clear out the cottage garden."

"Really?" she asked, turning to Alec, and they were off. Lottie's vegetable garden at home had been the best in our street, and her marrows had often won prizes at the agricultural show. She loved all growing things, and I hoped the topic would distract her from the ghost train.

They talked about gardening the rest of the way home, and thankfully there were no further mentions of the ghost train. I hoped Lottie had forgotten about it. I didn't invite Alec in, for Lottie was looking pale and tired, and I could tell she wanted to return to bed.

"Forgive me, Jane?" he said as I saw him off at the gate.

"What for?" There were so many things.

"I don't want to fight with you. We're friends, yes?"

"Of course." He kissed my hand and I let him, although a multitude of conflicting feelings were swirling in my chest as I watched him leave. I'd thought I knew what I wanted from Alec, but now I wasn't so sure. Colleague, friend, lover, potential husband? If I was honest, I wasn't sure that 'husband' was something I really wanted ever again. But marrying Alec would provide some security for me, Lottie, and of course the baby.

Thinking about the baby drew my mind back to the strange conversation with Edith Carter. I hadn't mentioned it to Lottie yet, although I knew I probably should. I'd always thought Dr Carter to be a straight-laced, upright man, not the kind to break the law in such a way. He must truly believe he was providing a valuable service, to take such a risk. Why, if he were found out, the consequences would be dire.

And suddenly something clicked, and the pieces fell together in my mind. I needed to know if I was right. I ran back into the house to tell Lottie where I was going, but she was already asleep. I scrawled a quick note for her and left it on the table, then grabbed my hat and headed back into town.

I arrived at the doctor's surgery panting, with my hair coming out of its bun and drifting around my face in untidy wisps. I stood on the step for a moment, trying to catch my breath, then turned the handle and entered.

"Mrs Adams," Edith said, rising from her desk with a look of concern. "Is it your sister? Shall I fetch my husband?"

"No," I said. "It's you I need to see."

"Me?"

"It's about what you told me today. The night Brian Mathieson died, is that where your husband was? Visiting a woman in trouble?"

She looked shocked for a moment, then nodded.

"But there's no way that woman will testify as such to the police, is there?"

Edith laughed mirthlessly. "Of course not. Would you?"

"And the night John Anderson was poisoned, what was Doctor Carter doing when he left the table?"

"I was simply using the facilities, as I already told Constable Ward. One of the maids saw me." The doctor strode into the room through the door behind me. "So, you know about my other work, do you?"

"I do."

"And what will you do with that information?"

"You know I have to tell Constable Ward—unless you'd rather be tried for murder?"

"There are some who say I should be regardless."

I shrugged. "That's none of my business. Our job is to find out who killed Brian Mathieson and poisoned John Anderson, and why."

"Well, it wasn't me." He turned and marched back into his office, slamming the door. Edith stared at the desk.

"I should go," I said.

"Will...will David be in any trouble?" she asked, peering up at me, mouse-like.

"I don't know. But I'll do my best for him now that I know the truth," I said. It never hurt to cultivate a sense of gratitude in people like Edith. I might need her one of these days. She grabbed my hand.

"Thank you," she whispered, and I saw the glint of tears in her eyes. I mumbled something appropriate and extricated myself, feeling uncomfortable.

I took the walk home much more slowly, for I needed time to think. It was a golden afternoon, and the whole world looked rosy. But I barely noticed the scenery; I was too preoccupied. So there was no way that David Carter could have killed Brian, but he and Peter Maloney could still have got someone else to do it. Finding out about the doctor's real whereabouts hadn't actually damaged my theory at all. He could still have poisoned John Anderson, or arranged to have had it done.

Lottie was still asleep when I got home, so I made myself some dinner and left a plate of bread and cheese by the bed in case she woke hungry. I ate on the verandah in the dusk, mulling things over, and came to a decision. Alec had made it clear he wanted proof that Peter Maloney was involved in Brian's death before he'd take any action. So I'd just have to find some. The thought sustained me as I readied myself for bed, and I drifted off to sleep still making plans.

CHAPTER 16

When I woke it was deep night and unseasonably cold. I rolled over to snuggle up to Lottie's warm bulk, but my arm hit bare sheets, startling me out of my half-doze. I sat up, fumbling for the candle and matches that I always left beside the bed. When I finally found them, the light confirmed it: Lottie was gone. As I sat there puzzling, trying to get some sense out of my sluggish brain, I heard a familiar rumble along the tracks that ran beside the cottage. My blood tingled as if it had turned to iced water, for it could only mean one thing. The ghost train had returned.

I stumbled out of bed, pulling a thick woollen shawl over my nightclothes and almost overturning the candle in my haste. The only thing I could think about was that I needed to find Lottie before she saw the train, for it would surely frighten her terribly. I hurried to the kitchen, calling her name, but I got no response. There was a candle burning on the table with an open book beside it; she must have been unable to sleep and had come out here to read.

Outside, the cool night air woke me as effectively as a pail of water to the face. I hurried along the verandah, but Lottie wasn't there. It wasn't until I reached the end of the verandah and glanced along the railway line that I saw her. She was standing beside the tracks, far too close for my liking, peering down towards where the spectral train was rumbling ever closer. I leapt down the steps and hurried through the gate towards her.

"Lottie!" I called out. "What are you doing?" She turned and saw me, or perhaps she just recognised my voice.

"It's all right," she called back. "I just wanted to see it for myself." She sounded unusually brave, but it wasn't all right, not to me. I remembered the apparently ghostly driver, and the terror that had sent me tearing back into the house to bury my face in my blankets. I had to protect her from that.

"Don't look at it!" I yelled as the train thundered closer, but it was too late; before I could reach her it was upon us.

"Jane!" she called, "I can see it! It's not a ghost!" But the word 'ghost' was cut short as something flew from the train's cabin and hit Lottie squarely in the head. She crumpled like a rag-doll. I screamed and ran to her, pulling her back from the line as the train tore past and vanished into the distance. Suddenly all was deathly quiet.

"Lottie!" I cried, shaking her. "Wake up! Please wake up!" There was a nasty gash on her head, with blood pouring from the wound. I pulled off my shawl and tried to staunch the flow with it as best I could. She was still breathing, but she wouldn't respond to my entreaties.

"Help!" I screamed, hoping someone would hear me, although there were few houses around these parts. "Please help me!" I didn't know what to do; I couldn't leave Lottie here in this state, her blood pooling over the stones beside the track. I wasn't usually the praying kind, but at that moment I begged for someone to hear me.

Miraculously, someone did, for I could hear footsteps pounding down the road. "Help!" I called again. "Quickly!" Moments later George Bailey, the stationmaster, was beside me; his house was just behind the station, and he must have heard my cry. He was still wearing his uniform, which was odd at that time of night, but I hardly noticed.

"What's happened?" he asked.

"It was the ghost train," I babbled. "Something hit her in the head. Please fetch the doctor!"

"I'll go right away," he said, not stopping to ask questions, and for the first time since we met I was grateful to him.

I pulled Lottie close to me, still pressing my shawl against the terrible wound. The material was already stained red. "Stay with me," I whispered, trying to hold back my tears. "Help will be here soon, I promise. Everything will be all right." She didn't move or give any indication that she'd heard.

The wait seemed interminable. I didn't know if it was minutes or hours, for I slipped into a kind of daze, where all I was conscious of was myself and Lottie, sitting there together, as if in a bubble cut out of the world.

Just when I began to think it was hopeless, I heard the thump of a horse's hooves and the crunch of cart wheels. There was a "whoa, there," as the cart pulled up, and a flash of lantern-light, and then Dr Carter was there beside me, and with him was Alec.

"What happened?" the doctor demanded.

"Something hit her," I mumbled, my teeth chattering. I was unaware until now how cold I'd become. Dr Carter grunted, but he didn't waste time investigating the particulars.

"Hold the lamp up a bit, Constable," he said to Alec, then unwrapped my shawl and probed the wound. My vision clouded and I felt sick.

"We need to get her out of the night air," he said. "You too, Mrs Adams. We'll take her to your house; it's closest." He grabbed a plank out of the bed of the cart and between them, he and Alec manoeuvred Lottie's unconscious form onto it. I felt like I was in a bad dream.

"She's pregnant, yes?" the doctor asked as they carried Lottie inside and laid her on the bed. I nodded. It didn't seem to matter now who knew.

"How far along?"

"Three months or so."

"Constable Ward, take Mrs Adams to the kitchen and make her a cup of tea," the doctor instructed. "She needs to warm up. Put plenty of sugar in it." I let Alec lead me to the kitchen, where he stoked the fire and set the kettle to boil. I sat at the table, but I couldn't stop shivering. I wished I could wake up from this nightmare.

"What exactly happened?" he asked as he filled the teapot. "What was she doing out there in the middle of the night?"

"It was the ghost train," I said, pressing my hands between my knees to stop them shaking. "She couldn't sleep and she went out to see it. I woke up and couldn't find her, and then I saw her standing there as the train went by. Something flew out from the train and hit her, and she fell." My voice cracked, and I swallowed. Alec put a cup of tea in front of me and I wrapped my hands around it, hunching over it as if it would protect me.

"Did she say anything?"

"She called out that she could see it and that it wasn't a ghost," I said numbly. "I don't know what she meant."

"Did she mean she could see a person on the train?"

I shrugged, for I had no answers for him. We sat in silence for some time, for words seemed useless now. All that was left was to wait.

Time seemed to be moving in strange ways; I no longer had any concept of hours. All I knew was that at some point during that endless night the doctor returned, his face grave. I scrambled to my feet.

"Is she all right? She's going to be fine, isn't she?"

Dr Carter rubbed his eyes; he looked tired and careworn. "I think she'll recover," he said. "But," he added, clearly seeing the relief that rushed through me at his words, "I can't guarantee what sort of state she'll be in when she wakes. It was a nasty injury and it's hard to tell if there'll be any permanent damage. And I'm very sorry, Mrs Adams, but I'm afraid she's lost the baby."

I couldn't quite believe this, for all along I hadn't even contemplated that Lottie's unborn child might not survive. "How can this be?"

The doctor shook his head. "The shock, the cold, the way she fell...and sometimes these things just happen," he said. "I'll send Edith along in the morning to help you take care of her." I nodded, knowing from bitter experience exactly what my darling sister would be going through.

There was a clatter of boots on the steps then, and a ragged boy poked his head into the kitchen. I vaguely recognised him as one of the children of some itinerant labourers who were passing through. "They said you'd be here, Doctor," he panted. "Me mam's baby's comin' and they sent me to fetch yer."

"I have to go," the doctor said, packing up his bag. "I'll call in the morning to see how she is." He squeezed my hand briefly—an unexpected gesture of kindness from this otherwise taciturn man—and then he was gone.

It was only as the door closed behind him that the shock hit me all over again. My knees gave way and I crumpled to the floor, shaking. I liked to think I was strong enough for anything, but Lottie had always held a tender place in my heart. Sobs welled up in my chest and burst forth, almost choking me.

"Jane," Alec said, kneeling beside me, his arms around my shoulders. "It's all right, Jane. It's going to be all right." I leaned against him for a moment, but I couldn't maintain the illusion. Things were never going to be all right again, and it was partly his fault.

"You did this," I hissed. "You should never have told her about the ghost train."

"Come on, Jane, be reasonable," he said gently. "You've had a terrible shock, but this is no one's fault."

"You only did it to laugh at me, and if you hadn't told her, she wouldn't have gone looking for it!" I snapped back. "I was trying to protect her from it!"

"That's unfair," he said, looking hurt. "She would have found out eventually; you know she would. And if anyone's to blame, I'd say it's the person who threw that rock!"

He was right, and I knew it. And at that moment I could feel my tears drying into a cold fury. "I'm going to find them," I said with all the intensity of a vow. "I'm going to find them and make them wish they'd never been born."

Alec seemed taken aback by this; he'd never heard me speak like that before, for I'd always contained myself around him. But nobody hurt my family and got away with it. I would spend the rest of my life hunting them if I had to.

"What are you going to do?" he asked, sounding somewhat wary.

"I'm going to find that ghost train," I said. "Will you help me?"

He sighed. "It certainly seems to have got out of control," he said. "And I don't believe it's a ghost any more than we are. I think it's time we unmasked it. So yes, I'll help you."

I scrambled to my feet and went to the bedroom, where my sister lay unmoving. The doctor had bandaged her head, but she looked wan and terribly frail. I crawled onto the bed next to her, laying my face beside hers.

"I promise I'll find who did this," I whispered in her ear. "I'll find them, and I'll make them pay."

CHAPTER 17

I must have fallen asleep lying there beside Lottie, for the next thing I knew, somebody was shaking me awake. I sat up groggily, wondering for a moment where I was, before it all came back to me. I'd hoped it was just a horrible dream, but one look at my sister's bandaged head and I knew it wasn't.

Dr Carter and Edith were standing by the bed. They didn't say much—Edith just helped me to the kitchen, where she made tea and boiled some eggs for breakfast. I wondered dimly where the eggs had come from, for poor old Estella hadn't been laying properly since Bertha died, but then I noticed the basket of food on the table. Edith must have brought it with her. I'd never really thought much about the doctor's mousy, unassuming little wife—to me she'd always just been another of Grace's hangers-on—but she clearly knew how to comfort someone under duress.

"Here," Edith said, setting an egg and a plate of toast in front of me. "You need to eat." I picked at the food without much appetite, although I knew she was right. I didn't know how long we stayed sitting at the table; it could have been minutes or hours. There was no sign of Alec. He must have left after I'd fallen asleep.

I was roused from my torpor by Dr Carter entering the kitchen. He looked hopeful, which I took as a positive sign.

"Some good news," he said. "Your sister is awake."

The flood of relief in my chest was so great I feared it would stop my heart. I jumped to my feet. "And she's all right?"

Dr Carter looked grave. "She's...not quite what she was, at least not yet." He gestured to the door. "Come and see her, if you like."

I followed him down the hall to the bedroom, unsure whether to laugh or cry. I wanted to castigate Lottie for giving us all such a fright, but overwhelmingly I was just glad to have her back. Then I saw her.

The doctor was right—she was awake. But she just looked blankly around the room without recognition, and when I softly called her name she didn't respond.

"Why isn't she speaking?"

"It could be a combination of the fright and the injury," Dr Carter said. "I really don't know at this point."

"Will she get better?"

"She might...but I can't guarantee it."

"No..." I whispered. Seeing my beautiful, vivacious sister reduced to this was almost too much to bear. But I couldn't afford to break down. Lottie would need me to fight for her now more than ever.

Dr Carter had other patients to see, so he left shortly afterwards, promising to return in the evening, but Edith stayed with me. If Lottie was aware of what was happening to her in the aftermath of losing her baby, she seemed unconcerned by it. We took care of her as best we could, and when we offered her food she ate listlessly, but she didn't seem to taste it. I went through the motions, feeling like I was watching myself from above. It didn't seem quite real.

The following days and weeks soon fell into a familiar pattern. The doctor came twice a day to check Lottie's wounds, and Edith was a near-constant, quiet presence, helping me do whatever needed to be done. We tended not to talk much, for I increasingly found solace in silence. Too much conversation would make it seem like things were returning to normal, when it couldn't be further from the truth. Lottie's physical injuries healed quite quickly, but she was no longer who she used to be. The joyful, whip-smart girl was gone, leaving in her place this dazed, silent stranger.

Of course, news of the accident spread quickly through the town, and I now faced a constant stream of visitors. I accepted their food but declined their company for any longer than strict politeness required; after all, they'd never wanted anything to do with me before I became such a rich source of gossip. This town fed off drama like leeches did blood.

Alec called most days, but I didn't want to see him either. I couldn't shake the feeling that none of this would have happened if he hadn't told Lottie about the ghost train.

Coupled with the doubts I'd already been having over the bushranger incident, my trust in him had been badly damaged.

Lottie's condition improved as the weeks passed, and she needed less-frequent care, for she was docile and compliant, although sometimes inclined to wander. If Edith wasn't with me—and she was coming less and less as the immediate need receded—I had to lock Lottie in the bedroom while I went to work. I started to worry about how we were going to manage in the long term, for my capacity to work would be limited if I had to care for her all the time, and I couldn't afford to employ anyone to help me. I needed money, for I refused to rely any more than I had to on the kindness of strangers. But contacting my parents was impossible after everything that had happened, and I wasn't in touch with any of my brothers or other relations.

Unable to solve that problem immediately, I began brooding more and more on the ghost train. I didn't for a minute believe it was spectral: someone or something was behind it, and I was determined to find out who or what it was. I needed to understand what had happened to Lottie and why.

I thought about my original theory that the train was being run by a group of railway men. Lottie's arrival had put paid to my plan to get hold of the stationmaster's roster, but I felt that now was the time to revisit it.

And so, on a soft summer's night when not a breath of wind stirred the trees, I snuck out of the house and up to the station. I was nervous about leaving Lottie alone, but she was fast asleep and, in any case, I didn't plan to be gone long.

The station, so quaint in the daylight, was rather eerie beneath the moon. Its proportions seemed slightly wrong somehow, and the shadows pooled in inky wells under the eaves. Each step I took along the platform echoed loudly in my ears, until I was sure I'd wake the whole town, or at least Mr Bailey in his little house behind the station.

I was grateful to find that, even after all this time, he still hadn't fixed the window I'd tampered with. Most probably it had been too hot to close it during the day and he hadn't even noticed. I lifted the sash, jumping nervously as it creaked and groaned. Finally I'd opened a wide enough space for me to crawl through, and I hitched up my skirts and slithered inside. I hadn't brought a lantern because the moon was almost full, but it took my eyes a while to adjust to the darkness of the office, and I swore as I stumbled against the desk. My heart pounded in my ears as I glanced frantically around the room, looking for the most logical place to keep a roster. There wasn't a lot of choice, for the office was quite sparsely furnished, and I quickly hit on the desk drawer as the most likely spot. Unfortunately, when I tried it, it was locked. I cursed to myself and set about trying to find the key. I hoped Mr Bailey hadn't taken it with him.

I was scouring the bookcase when the window sash slipped and fell closed with an almighty crash. My heart began racing so fast it felt like it was trying to crawl up my throat. Luckily, the glass in the window was intact, and I could only hope the noise hadn't been noticed.

I was beginning to think I'd got away with it when I heard the scrunch of footsteps on the platform outside. I ducked down below the level of the window as a beam of lantern light cut through, and I heard Mr Bailey's raspy breathing. I held my own breath, praying that he wouldn't open the door.

Thankfully, something was on my side, for although the lantern passed by again, nobody tried the door. Even so, I stayed crouched on the floor for a good long time after he'd gone, just to be sure. When I eventually got the courage to move, I returned to the bookcase, and there I saw it, glinting in the moonlight: a small brass key lying on the shelf. I tried it in the desk drawer and, sure enough, it turned. I briefly wondered why Mr Bailey even bothered to lock the drawer if he was just going to leave the key lying around.

I opened the drawer to reveal a stack of papers and a small bottle of whisky, half-full. I had no doubt that this was the truly valuable thing, in Mr Bailey's eyes at least, and the real reason for his security measures, such as they were. I rifled through the papers, squinting to make out the writing in the semi-darkness. I was starting to lose hope when, towards the bottom, I found it—the roster. It was laid out with dates and times, and the names of the men working the various roles on the trains. I looked up the date of Lottie's encounter with the ghost train and noted the names, then found the dates of the other two nights I'd seen it. As I'd suspected, the names were all the same. I flicked quickly back through the pages, but those names didn't appear together on any other nights over the time I'd been in Tungold. Then I glanced forward; the next time they were rostered on simultaneously was in three nights' time. The roster continued for another month and then ended; there was no telling when they'd be on together again, and I'd have to repeat this whole exercise to find out. It was now or never.

I desperately wanted to take a copy of the roster with me, but there was only one in the drawer and I didn't have the time or resources to copy it. I'd already been there much longer than I'd intended, and if Mr Bailey caught me I'd be in all sorts of trouble. It was time to go. I tucked the papers and the bottle back into the drawer in the order in which I'd found them, locked it and returned the key to its place in the bookcase. Then I lifted the window sash carefully and squeezed out. There was a moment of panic when it began to slip again, but I caught it in time. Even so, it was all I could do to stop myself running back along the platform and instead walk calmly and quietly. Once I was sure I was out of earshot of the stationmaster's house I gave vent to my feelings and dashed down the road, not stopping until I reached the safety of my own verandah. Lottie was thankfully still sound asleep when I entered the bedroom, and if she'd woken while I'd been gone and missed me, she showed no sign of it. I undressed and crawled into bed beside her, but it took some time for my heart to stop pounding enough that sleep stood a chance. I wondered what I was going to tell Alec. I was tempted to leave him out of it entirely and just go hunting for the ghost train myself, but I wasn't completely stupid. I knew I needed help, and Alec was really the only person in a position to offer it. For one thing, he had a gun.

I woke the next morning groggy and tired, but triumphant. Lottie was in good spirits too, smiley and compliant, which relieved me, for she was much more given to sudden mood changes these days and could easily become distressed. I was tempted to walk into town, but Lottie was so peaceful that I couldn't bear to shake her out of it—crowds, even the small crowds at the Tungold shops, frightened her—and I couldn't very well leave her at home by herself again. But I needed to tell Alec what I knew.

As fate would have it, the object of my thoughts walked in at the gate as I was sitting with my morning cup of tea on the verandah. We hadn't really talked properly since the night of Lottie's accident, but today I was glad to see him.

"You're looking well," he said. My enthusiasm must have shown on my face.

"I think I've cracked it," I said without preamble. "The ghost train—I think I know how we can find it."

"Really?"

"I've found the common factor. It only runs when certain people are rostered on at the same time. All we have to do is wait for the next time they're on together and follow it back to wherever it goes."

"How on earth did you discover that?"

"I followed a hunch."

"But how...You know, I don't think I really want to know."

"A wise choice. Just take my word for it."

"And you're sure you really want to do this? It sounds a little bit mad, following a ghost train."

I scowled at him, for I'd been hoping for more support. "If you don't want to come, I'll go on my own," I said. "I'm going to figure it out one way or another, and I'm not overly bothered if you're with me or not." He looked hurt at my words, but I didn't care. I'd finished playing games. These people, whoever they were, had hurt my sister, and I would find them. And heaven help them when I did.

"When are you planning to go?"

"The night after tomorrow. It may very well be our last chance. Are you in?"

He thought about it for a moment. "Of course I am."

"Good," I said. "Meet me here at eleven o'clock and we'll see what we can find."

CHAPTER 18

I was on edge for the next two days, itching to get on with our hunt. I worried that the ghost train wouldn't appear, or that I'd be otherwise disappointed, but all I could do was wait. I fretted about what to do about Lottie, and finally decided to wait until she was sleeping and then lock the bedroom door. She went to bed early these days and always slept through the night, often not waking until nine or ten o'clock the next day. I was confident that she'd be fine if I was away for a few hours.

When the rostered night finally came I forced myself to eat some dinner, although my stomach was churning so fiercely I was afraid I wouldn't be able to keep it down. I passed the time until Alec arrived by pacing around the kitchen. When he knocked at the door I almost jumped out of my skin, I was wound so tightly. The first thing I noticed was the revolver holstered at his hip.

"Ready?" he asked. He looked as apprehensive as I felt.

"As ready as I'll ever be," I said. "Where do you think we should wait?"

"I suggest we go round to the railway side of the cottage and wait there," he said. "We'll be hidden in the shadow of the verandah. But are you sure the train will return to its hiding place?"

I sighed. "No," I said. "I'm not sure at all. I don't even really understand what it is we're tracking. But it must go somewhere, and it'd make sense to run it as few nights as possible—less chance of being seen." I looked at him, suddenly worried he was going to back out on me. For all my talk of going alone, I was glad of his company. "You're not having second thoughts, are you?"

He grinned. "Of course not. This is the most exciting police work I've done since I came to Tungold." But there was something in the way he looked at me that made me wonder. What wasn't he telling me?

I dressed warmly—because now that autumn was on the way the temperature was starting to drop at night—and made sure to put on my sturdy boots. Our preparations made, we sat at the kitchen table in silence, waiting for the telltale thump and clatter of the ghost train. The clock on the dresser ticked audibly, and I had to stop myself from glancing at it constantly only to find the hands had barely moved. The time dragged ever so slowly, without a sound from the railway, and I began to question the wisdom of this venture. There was no guarantee the train would even come tonight, roster or no.

Slowly, inexorably, the hands of the clock ticked round past midnight. I stifled another yawn and wondered if I should just give it up and go to bed. Maybe my theory about the roster was wrong—maybe the train wouldn't be coming at all. And then I would have lost my chance, and Alec would think I was a fool to boot.

I was about to suggest we call it a night when I heard it—a low thrum of iron lines. Alec opened his mouth to say something but I held up my hand, still not quite sure if I was imagining it. But the rumbling got louder, eventually resolving itself into the rhythmic clacking of train wheels.

"This is it!" I exclaimed. We jumped up so fast that I nearly overturned my chair in my haste. Alec grabbed his satchel and we hurried out onto the verandah. I blew out the candle on the kitchen table as we went, leaving the house in darkness.

Running down the steps and around the far end of the verandah reminded me vividly of that first terrifying night I'd encountered the ghost train. I felt the familiar flutter of fear in my belly, but at least this time I knew what to expect. Sure enough, when the glowing spectre appeared I felt not so much a flash of terror as a flood of relief. I finally had a chance to solve this mystery.

I crouched down below the verandah rail—although I was sure it was too dark for anyone in the train to see me anyhow—and Alec joined me.

"Now what?" he whispered. It surprised me that he seemed to see me as the leader of this escapade.

"Let's follow it," I said. "It can't go all that far, not if it needs to be hidden by sunup. And I want to know where it's going."

"What do you suggest, then?"

"We need to be there when it stops," I said. "Look." The train was rumbling slowly past us now, and I pointed to the covered wagon it was towing. It had no other carriages—just the locomotive and the wagon. "We're going to hitch a ride on that."

He looked at me like I was mad, but said nothing.

We left the verandah and walked alongside the railway line, following the train in the direction of the station. It was visible now only as a faint glow in the moonlight, but I could still hear the metallic singing of the lines, which reassured me. Then the thrumming stopped.

"Quickly!" I hissed to Alec, and we increased our pace. I stumbled, causing a small cascade of stones, which rattled frighteningly loudly in the still night air.

The train had stopped at the station, so we crouched down in the shadow of the platform and watched. Three men were busy loading boxes and sacks into the wagon. One turned, and I gasped as his face caught the moonlight: it was the stationmaster, George Bailey. I thought about the night of Lottie's accident, and how Mr Bailey had been the first to arrive, still in his uniform although it had been well after midnight. I was shaken, because this was the first proper confirmation I'd had that he was involved in whatever nefarious business was going on. It made sense, really; it must have been much easier to run an illicit train with the stationmaster's cooperation. I wondered what was in the boxes and sacks they were loading. From a distance they looked like the kind of bags one would keep food and other perishable stores in.

It wasn't long before the final sacks were loaded and the men began readying the locomotive for departure. I saw our chance and tugged at Alec's sleeve.

"Come on, let's go!" I didn't wait for his response, but started forward. The men were all concentrating on the locomotive and didn't see us darting past in the dark. We reached the back of the wagon and I clambered up. There was a tearing noise as my skirt caught on a hook, but I didn't have time to worry about that. Alec scrambled up behind me.

The wagon was mostly empty, apart from the stores, and the men had replaced its tarpaulin cover. We slid in underneath and lay flat on the bed of the truck, the tarpaulin just a few inches from our faces. There was a jolt, then a hiss of steam and the screech of steel as the train moved forward. I wondered again why these men had chosen to use a train, for it wasn't exactly a subtle form of transport. But then, apart from me and the stationmaster, nobody lived close to the railway line. And if Mr Bailey was in on it, then I was the only liability.

The train travelled slowly for the first few minutes, but it picked up speed soon enough, presumably once it was clear of the town. I wondered where we were headed, for I'd been led to believe that the railway line was impassable further down, thanks to the old accident. Now that we were moving and there was no chance of being seen by the locomotive driver, I sat up and unhooked part of the tarpaulin, peering out into the darkness. But all was wilderness and I couldn't get my bearings. It was only the change in the gradient—for the train began to slow as we went downhill—that told me we must be heading over the escarpment.

"What can you see?" Alec asked. The train was too noisy for us to even bother trying to whisper.

"Nothing," I said, quite truthfully. "Just trees." I looked at him but couldn't make out his expression in the dark. I crawled back and crouched down again. I almost wanted to take Alec's hand, but decided against it, thinking of those same fingers on the trigger of his gun, pressed against Captain Starlight's head.

I didn't know how long the journey through the darkness had taken, but it had begun to feel like we'd been on the train forever. The rhythm of the wheels lulled me into a trance, and I even started to wonder whether it *was* in fact a ghost train and we'd doomed ourselves to riding it in this purgatory for eternity. But eventually the train began to slow down, as if it was drawing into a station.

I pulled up a corner of the tarpaulin again to see if I could work out what was happening. Alec sat up next to me and together we peeked out as the train shuddered and drew to a stop. I expected it to be dark, but there was the warm glow of torchlight. My stomach churned with anticipation.

"We'd better get down," Alec whispered in my ear, his lips brushing my hair. "We don't want to be caught here." I nodded, although I was unsure if he could see me.

Carefully, he peered under the edge of the tarpaulin at the back of the wagon. "All clear," he muttered, then slithered down. I followed suit, Alec catching my ankles as I descended. We ducked down behind the wagon, taking stock of our surroundings.

The train appeared to have stopped in the middle of the forest, without a station or any other convenience in sight, save for a long torch stuck into the stones at the side of the track. All around us was dense bush. We must have been beyond the edge of the escarpment, but we clearly hadn't yet entered the wide pastoral country that surrounded

Queensgrace on the other side. The bush on either side rose steeply away from the railway line.

As we watched, two men descended from the locomotive and walked towards the torch. When they reached it, they turned up the hill into the trees, as if treading a well-known path. As soon as they were far enough away that they wouldn't be able to see us, I started forward, ignoring Alec's muffled cry of surprise. I knew it was risky, for we couldn't be sure that there weren't more men on the train, but I needed to know where they were going. Up in those hills was the explanation for what had happened to Lottie.

We reached the torch, and I saw a track leading off into the forest, made by the repeated passage of many feet. We followed it cautiously, for once we were beyond the torch's light it was difficult to see. Even the full moon had trouble penetrating the depths of bush as dense as this, and I worried one of us would twist an ankle. Thankfully, we made it up the hill without incident. The path was lit periodically by lanterns set on flat rocks—for torches among the undergrowth would have been far too dangerous—so we knew we were on the right track, but their light didn't extend far. We scuttled hurriedly past each lantern, both glad and fearful of its light. Our footsteps over the twigs and fallen leaves sounded abominably loud in the dark, and I was terrified we'd be heard. Every rustle of some small creature in the undergrowth caused me to jump. When Alec, behind me, stepped on a stick with a loud crack, I feared my heart would fly clean out of my chest.

The path began to peter out about halfway up the hill. By this time we were both puffing like engines and dripping with sweat, despite the night chill. As the ground flattened out a bit I saw another burst of light, this one much bigger. We crept closer and spotted two lanterns at the entrance of what appeared to be a cave, cut into the hillside and shored up with thick slabs of wood.

"It's a mine," Alec said in amazement. We shared a glance, not even having to consult on what to do next. He picked up a lantern, and together we entered the old tunnel.

The way into the mine was marked by narrow-gauge rails that I assumed were for carts that carried out whatever it was that was being dug up. There were no signs of any such carts, but the lines were shining and unbroken, as if they'd been recently used. The mine itself, though, appeared to be much older. Some of the timber supports looked unstable, while others had been reinforced with newer wood. Occasionally a small shower of dirt and stones trickled down from between the slabs.

We walked cautiously, not speaking, for up ahead the tracks bent in a wide loop and we couldn't see what lay beyond. As we got closer to the corner I paused, thinking I heard the faint echo of voices. Alec looked at me as if he was about to say something, but I placed a finger to my lips. We tiptoed slowly onwards, and the voices got gradually louder. There were several men speaking, I thought; the two from the train, probably, plus who knew how many more. For the first time since this whole ridiculous adventure began, I stopped to wonder what I'd got us into and, more importantly, how we were going to get out. But we were here now, and my curiosity was insatiable. I had to know what was going on.

We reached the bend and peered cautiously around, hugging the wall. There were five men, their faces covered with scarves against the dust and dirt. Three of them were dislodging lumps of whitish stone at the far end of the mine, while the other two inspected the stone then packed it into the small trucks standing on the rails. I could feel Alec close behind me.

"Quartz," he whispered. "They're looking for gold. They're shipping the ore out of here to be crushed and processed somewhere else." I didn't ask how he suddenly knew so much about mining.

I leaned a bit further forward, trying to see better, but I lost my balance and slipped, falling in a clatter of stones on metal. The clanging rang out like gunshots and the voices stopped abruptly. I could see Alec was torn between glancing down at me to see if I required assistance, and watching the bend in the tunnel. I inspected my left ankle, which had rolled under me as I fell, and probed it with my fingers, searching for any painful spots. It was only when I heard a familiar voice that I looked up.

"Well, well, Constable Ward. And Mrs Adams. This is the last place I expected to find you."

"Mr Maloney," Alec said evenly. I scrambled to my feet only to find Alec with his revolver drawn. Peter Maloney was standing maybe fifteen feet away, and he too had a gun—pointed at Alec's chest.

"You!" I exclaimed despite myself. "It was you all along!"

Maloney ignored me, still facing off with Alec. "What are you doing here, Constable?" he asked, his lip curling. "Always poking your nose in where it's not wanted." I noticed that three other men had emerged from the shadows to stand behind Peter. We were hopelessly outnumbered.

"If you have nothing to hide, my presence shouldn't alarm you," Alec said, his voice unwavering. I fought down a mad desire to laugh. We were in an old mine, having hitched a ride on a ghost train, and Peter Maloney was pointing a gun at us. It certainly looked like he had something to hide.

"You know, they say there's gold in these hills," Alec continued in the same conversational tone. "Lots of it, at one point, but it was difficult to get out and the mine closed down. Those old prospectors thought they'd got it all. But they hadn't, had they?"

Maloney tried to look casual, but he couldn't hide a small start of shock. He must have thought his operation was undetectable, but Alec had clearly been doing his research.

"But why keep it a secret?" Alec asked. "A gold rush could have made Tungold prosperous. Look at Ballarat and Bendigo and all those other towns. Queensgrace would have profited too. I would have thought that would be what you wanted?"

I realised then that Alec, civic-minded as he was, couldn't understand those with more base motives. Were Alec in Peter Maloney's situation, he probably would have publicised the find and then waited for the deluge of hopeful prospectors that would have ensured Tungold's future. But I could see why Peter had made the choice he did. By keeping it secret and only employing a few trusted associates, he'd made himself rich, and also indispensable to those that mattered. In Peter Maloney's philosophy, it was every man for himself. I admired Alec's community spirit, but, if I was completely honest, I identified more with Maloney. His way was more realistic, and I'd learned the hard way that you had to look out for yourself, because no one else would do it for you.

Maloney just laughed at Alec's comment, and I wondered if he saw him as naive, as I was inclined to. Much as I disliked the man, I had to admire the slickness of the operation.

"So you dig up the gold, then pack it up and ship it out on the train," Alec said, still with no response from Maloney. "Where did you get the train?"

"They 'borrow' it as they need it," I said, as the pieces finally fitted together in my mind. "They've got enough people in the right places who can turn blind eyes to a locomotive that isn't where it should be."

"Very good, young lady," Maloney said with a smirk. "You've got it all figured out, haven't you?"

"Not quite," I said honestly. "I still don't understand how you made the train appear so ghostly."

Maloney chuckled. "You can thank Charlie Chin for that," he said. "Them Chinese chappies know all about fireworks and all those sorts of things. He made us a paint that glows in the dark. It even had me fooled the first time I saw it. And then we just hose it off afterwards and no one is any the wiser." He seemed to be relaxing as he revelled in his achievements; the barrel of the gun was dropping slightly. Behind him, his cronies stood like statues. I didn't recognise any of them.

I decided to take a final chance. "And so when Brian Mathieson came to town threatening to clear the old line and extend the railway, you were terrified he'd find this place," I said. "So you killed him and tried to poison John Anderson as well just to be sure."

"Now wait just a minute..." Maloney began, but Alec jumped in first.

"I think it's best if you come along quietly, Mr Maloney..." But he didn't get to finish his sentence before there was the crack of a gunshot in the tunnel. I instinctively crashed to the ground as a second shot rang out. When the smoke cleared, I looked around me, dazed. The echo of the shots was still ringing in my ears. My palms were grazed from where they'd hit the stony ground, and the acrid stench of gunpowder filled my nostrils. Alec was lying a little way from me, but as I watched he sat up, apparently unhurt. The same couldn't be said for Peter Maloney. Both men must have fired their guns, but whereas Maloney's bullet had missed, Alec's had taken the squatter clean through the head. It was obvious he was dead. His three companions were cowering back against the wall in horror.

"What did you do that for?" I yelled irrationally at Alec. Somehow I felt that by killing Peter Maloney he'd done me out of any chance of justice for Lottie. It was clear to me now what had happened—someone in the train had panicked upon seeing her watching them and had thrown something at her. I thought of Lily Jacobs, who'd died in similar circumstances, the exact truth of which we'd now never know.

"You should have arrested him, not shot him!" I yelled again. I could feel my reason slipping away in a flash of rage. "He killed Brian Mathieson!"

"No, he didn't, Jane," Alec said quietly. The calmness in his voice brought me back to myself and I felt a terrible lurch in my guts.

"What do you mean?"

"Peter Maloney didn't kill Brian Mathieson, and he didn't poison John Anderson. You did."

CHAPTER 19

I opened my mouth but nothing came out.

"And Brian wasn't the first, was he?" Alec said, a harshness in his eyes that I didn't recognise. "Tell me what happened to Jim."

"It was an accident," I whispered. My hands started to tremble. How long had he known? Had he just been using me all along? I fell to my knees, afraid I was about to be sick. I wanted to forget it all; I'd come to Tungold to forget it all, but still it had followed me.

The thing was, Jim's death truly had been an accident of sorts. He'd come home, drunk as usual, and despite my best efforts I must have looked at him wrong, because he'd started laying into me, first with his words and then with his fists. I could feel my mind separating from my body; it was like I was watching the whole thing from above. I didn't know where I found the strength, but I'd run—out the door of the cottage and along the embankment that rose above the railway cutting. I didn't know why I'd chosen to go that way, for it made no sense, but that was where I went.

He'd followed me. Bellowing like a bull, he was, and I'd known it would only be a matter of time before he caught me. And I'd been right. He'd caught up to me and gone to lay into me again, but that time I'd fought back, and we'd struggled on the edge of the embankment. His back was to the drop, and before I'd even realised what was happening, he'd stumbled backwards, slipping.

I'd made a choice then, even if it was an unconscious one. It would have been so easy to reach out and pull him back, to implore him to hold on while I struggled to balance his weight. But I didn't. Instead, I'd reached out towards him...and shoved him hard in the chest.

He'd stumbled backwards, his eyes widening as he realised what I'd done. His arms spun like windmills, beating the air, trying to find a purchase that wasn't there. And then he'd fallen, until he crashed onto the railway line below. He hadn't even had time to cry out.

I hadn't gone down to check if he was still alive. I'd contemplated it for a moment, but if he was, I couldn't bear to see it. I'd stumbled away from the terrible drop and vomited my guts up into a nearby bush. I hadn't intended to kill him—but if I hadn't, I would probably have been the dead one, if not that night then sooner or later. When there was nothing left to come up from my stomach but bile, I'd walked back to the cottage as if in a dream and crawled, shaking, into bed. None of it had felt real.

It had become real the next morning, when a policeman knocked on my door. I was still dazed and could hardly comprehend it when he'd told me Jim was dead, for I'd begun to think I'd dreamed the whole thing. I'd asked if I could see him but was told no; the 6.05 express had been by and had been unable to stop. I'd very nearly been sick again when I'd heard that. They'd asked if I knew why he would have been up on the cutting at that time of night and I'd told them I had no idea, that he often went to the pub of an evening and may have been drunk and lost his way in the dark. The officer had looked at my bruises and had doubtless drawn his own conclusions.

The funeral was a small affair. Some of Jim's railway mates were there, and his parents. Although our parents had refused to attend, Lottie had come with me, clutching my hand as if she was afraid I'd run away or fall to the ground sobbing or otherwise behave inappropriately. But I hadn't; I'd cried just the right amount. Enough to keep me from appearing cold, but not enough that I'd be pegged as some deranged female. In truth, they'd been tears of relief more than mourning, but no one else had needed to know that.

I'd stared at Jim's parents across the grave of their son, his father big and beefy with his flushed cheeks and breath stinking of booze, even at such an early hour of the day, and his mother, a tiny churchmouse of a woman, so insignificant as to be almost a shadow. I'd wondered if she knew how much her son had taken after his father, but when our eyes had locked across the great gaping hole in the graveyard, I'd realised she did and probably always had. From the moment

I'd met her, before the wedding, I had thought her weak and timid to a fault; I hadn't realised then that she moved with the delicacy of one hiding her own bruises. She'd looked at me with something I reflected on later to be a mixture of hope and fear: hope that my life would be different to hers, and fear that it wouldn't. Now, meeting again under such circumstances, I'd been able to smile at her through my tears, and had received a small, sad smile in return, full of shared regrets. Lottie had intercepted it but didn't understand, and I'd prayed she never would.

They think it starts suddenly, those people who have never had their identity stripped away by another, piece by piece, until there's nothing left but a broken shell of who they once were. They think that one day he hits you and from that moment on you're cowed and broken. They don't understand that you don't have to hit a person to destroy them; that the physical violence is often the end, not the beginning—for some women, quite literally, as it nearly was for me. They don't understand the choice I made.

After it was all over, moving away had seemed like the best option, and when I was offered the job in Tungold, I'd taken it gladly. The chance of a new start, without Jim and all the pain, had been irresistible. I could be anything I wanted to be; I could be the woman I might have been had I not let Jim roll me in the hay that day and ended up pregnant and forced into marriage at sixteen. It had all been for nothing anyway, for barely two months later I'd lost the baby, but by then Jim had already been starting to show his true colours and it was too late.

And it all would have been perfect, if Brian Mathieson hadn't shown up and stuck his nose into places where it didn't belong. He'd always had his suspicions, I think, although how he'd come about them I didn't know. But he was always turning up at the cottage in the wake of Jim's death, and on more than one occasion his advances had made me uncomfortable. I'd told him in no uncertain terms to get out and never return, and I think from that day onwards he'd taken against me. It may indeed have been a coincidence that he'd come to Tungold at the same time I had, but even if it was, he'd never been one to let an opportunity slip through his fingers. But Jim's death—and indeed the life I'd led with him—had changed me, made me tougher. I was capable of things I never had been before, but Brian wasn't to know that. At least, not until it was too late.

I hadn't actually intended to kill him either. I went to his room at the Tungold Hotel that night partly to ask him about the ghost train, but mainly to try to find out what he knew about Jim's death, and what it would take for him to keep quiet, for if he reported me I'd surely hang. I'd snuck in the back way so as not to be spotted by Annie or any of the staff, and climbed the stairs to his room. He'd looked surprised to see me when he opened the door.

"What are you doing here?" Brian wasn't known for his politeness, and his tone had been blunt.

"I was thinking about what you said this afternoon," I'd said. "About Jim."

"You'd best come in then." He'd looked me up and down as if I were some sort of delicacy he was about to devour. I knew this type of man well; the kind that saw women as playthings, as something less than human. It was a distasteful trait often overlaid with charm, as it had been with Jim, but although I'd fallen for it at sixteen, I was older and wiser now.

"Tell me what you know about his death," I'd said with no preamble. I had no intention of negotiating.

"Well now, what's it worth to you?"

"What do you want?"

He'd crossed the room and stroked my cheek slowly, intimately. I'd fought down the bile rising in my throat.

"I know you're not telling the truth, Jane," he'd said, lingering on my name. "And I know that naughty little girls who tell lies ought to be punished." Unable to help myself, I'd stepped back from him. But he didn't know that I'd come prepared. I'd been a victim before, but I never would be again.

"Tell me what you know," I'd said again, more forcefully this time.

"It wasn't an accident, was it, Jane?" he'd said. "And if they find out, you'll hang. But I'm a generous man and I won't tell. I'm sure we can come to some sort of...arrangement."

I'd reached into the folds of my skirts and withdrawn the large carving knife I'd secreted there. "I'm sure we can," I'd said, brandishing it at him. It wasn't what he'd been expecting; suddenly the power balance had shifted. He'd backed away from me, hands raised in front of him, palms out as if in surrender. Then he'd lunged at me, trying to take me by surprise. I'd swung the knife, cutting his hands. He didn't do it again.

I'd kept him walking backwards, out the doors and onto the wide balcony.

"The thing is," I'd said, "I can't trust you. I know the kinds of games men like you play. You'll tell me that you won't tell a soul, and then you'll run straight to the police and blab everything. So what's a girl to do?"

"I won't, I swear."

"Ah, but you were all keen to strike a bargain not five minutes ago. But I'm done bargaining for my life with men like you. This time, things will be different."

"You're insane, woman!"

"Perhaps. And whose fault is that?" I'd lunged at him with the knife, forcing him to step back until he was backed up against the balcony rail. He was a tall man and heavy, and the rail was low; the top of it only reached his backside. I'd got closer, forcing him to lean back over the rail, further and further. And then he'd leaned too far and gravity had done its work. His legs had slipped from under him and he'd gone toppling over the balcony rail to land with a sickening thud in the street. It wasn't a terribly long way to fall and I could still hear him groaning. Terrified, I'd run back downstairs and out the way I'd come, then all the way back to my cottage, where I'd flung myself fully clothed into bed. I didn't sleep a wink that night for fear of how it would all turn out. I hadn't seen the note on the desk; things had moved too fast and I'd had no idea about it until Alec had shown me the next day. After that, I'd just had to turn suspicion away from myself as best I could.

I was still crouched in the dirt like a cowering animal, Alec standing over me, all ruthless efficiency. Gone was the man who might once have loved me; in his place was a figure much more familiar. I wished I could explain why I'd done what I had, but I knew he wouldn't understand. This man who executed bushrangers in cold blood was surely incapable of such mercy.

"I know why you killed Brian, Jane," he said in that same harsh tone, although I hadn't said a word. "He could have exposed you. But John Anderson? Why him? Misdirection?"

I nodded. When people had started speculating about Brian's killer, it had been obvious that Peter Maloney was the main suspect. The railway connection had been clear for all to see. And then there'd been the matter of Brian's note: *J.A. murder.* He'd meant to throw suspicion onto me, of course, but it had been easy to put a different interpretation on it. Then I'd just needed evidence to back up my case. So when we'd visited Dr Carter to view Brian's body, I'd snuck back into his study while the men were in the morgue and Edith was fetching her stuffed parrot, and had stolen a vial of something I'd hoped would do the trick. At the dinner at the Andersons' it had been the work of a few moments to slip it into his food. I hadn't intended to kill him, although that would have added weight to my story, and I hadn't been all that sorry that he'd lived. The effect had been the same regardless.

"And poisoning yourself and pretending it was from the jam that Grace Maloney gave you—that was a stroke of genius. You almost had me fooled."

I hung my head. When Alec had started thinking that I might be the 'J.A.' referred to in the note, I'd had to make it clear that I was a victim, not the perpetrator. Peter had already made it easy by tormenting me with Bertha and the snakes after I'd started asking questions about the ghost train; this had been just one more thing I could lay at his feet. "How did you find out?" I whispered.

"Good old-fashioned police work," Alec said. "When you started trying to blame Peter Maloney at all costs I started to wonder what you were hiding, so I began looking into Jim's death."

"If you turn me in, I'll hang." I could feel tears beginning to run unchecked down my cheeks. "And what will happen to Lottie if I do?"

He sighed. "I cared for you, Jane, but no one is above the law."

"Have you no mercy?"

"Did you have any for those men?"

"Should I have had?"

He didn't answer this, just pulled me to my feet. His fingers caught in my hair, but I didn't cry out. He gestured to the three other men, who had been standing there the whole time in apparent shock at the death of their leader. Alec pulled a length of rope out of his police satchel and bound their hands, stringing them together into a chain gang. I waited for him to do the same to me, but he didn't. Perhaps he still had some vestige of compassion left.

"Right, all of you," he said. "Out we go." He marched us out in single file along the narrow tunnel, with the three roped-together men first, then me, with Alec following behind.

Outside, the sky had begun to lighten just enough that we could see where we were going. There was a damp pre-dawn chill in the air, fingers of which worked their way inside the folds of my clothes, freezing me to the bone. The light breeze was spicy with the scent of dew on the eucalyptus leaves.

Going down the hill was infinitely harder than going up; in the dark I hadn't realised how steep and rocky it was. We were above the railway line, the ghost train directly below us. I heard the thud of Alec's footsteps behind me, and occasionally felt the touch of his hand in the small of my back if he thought I was going too slowly. Once upon a time, that touch would have thrilled me; now I could only shudder. I thought about how I had once cared for him and wondered how I could have been so blind. I should have known that he, like every other man in my life, would eventually betray me. But this time that betrayal would end in my death. My destiny was not—never had been—my own.

Then I thought about Lottie, still in her catatonic state. What kind of life could she possibly have without me? Ma and Da might take care of her, but they wouldn't live forever, and they didn't love her like I did. They'd probably lock her away in some awful asylum where she'd never get to see the sun. And she would never have been in such a state to begin with if not for Alec terrorising her with tales of the ghost train. In a way, he would be responsible for both our deaths.

I stopped at this point, too blinded by tears of rage to go on. The path had bent around before its final descent to the railway line, and we were standing on an overhang about thirty feet above the locomotive.

"Keep moving," Alec said, his hand on my back.

"No," I said. I looked down at the other men, who were still picking their way down the incline, apparently unaware that we'd stopped. They looked gormless, leaderless, willing to follow anyone. I wondered how much of a cut in the mine's profits Peter Maloney had given them.

"I won't tell you again, Jane," Alec said, the hard edge back in his voice. "Move! Now."

"So you can kill me?" I spat, whipping round to face him. "Will you smile as they hang me?"

"Justice will be done," he says. "You're a murderer and a liar, and in my mind you deserve to swing. You're lucky I haven't shot you where you stand." The venom in his voice was astounding.

"So you *will* betray me, then?" I needed to be sure.

"I'll do what is right."

"Then so will I," I said. Lottie deserved more than a cell in an asylum, and I deserved more than a life shaped by vicious men. I moved closer to the edge of the overhang.

"Don't do it, Jane!" Alec yelled, reaching for me.

"It's not what you think," I said as we locked arms and I braced my weight against his. As I expected, he was unable to stop his momentum and went flying over the edge, landing with bone-shattering force on the locomotive's coal tender. His limbs were twisted at unnatural angles and blood gushed from a wound on his head. He didn't move.

"I'm sorry," I whispered, wiping away my tears. I turned away from Alec's broken body, feeling a momentary surge of regret at his fate, to confront the three gobsmacked miners.

Now that their leader was dead, fear was rippling through the men. I could see it in their eyes—they were rudderless. Chosen precisely because they were compliant fools, they were incapable of acting without orders, of thinking for themselves.

Alec had told me once that I'd make a good leader, that I shouldn't underestimate myself. An illicit gold mine probably wasn't what he'd had in mind, but he was no longer able to object.

I stepped out of the shadows into the growing light. "Right, lads," I said. "There's been a change of plan." A couple of them looked at me sceptically, but they stayed silent long enough for me to tell them my idea. And when I asked who was in, nobody protested. It seemed they'd rather follow me than no one at all. I knew that George Bailey would take some convincing, but I could be very persuasive.

As the ghost train puffed its way up the escarpment, I leaned out of the cabin and watched the old mine site recede from view. I had a feeling I'd get very familiar with this journey. It looked like I'd found my place in Tungold after all.

EPILOGUE

The young curate paused at the lychgate and checked his watch. He'd told Father John that he'd be there at one o'clock, but it had taken less time to walk from the station than he'd anticipated, and it was only just gone twelve-thirty. Reluctant to interrupt the priest at his lunch, the curate walked into the churchyard, set his suitcase on the church steps and wandered through the small graveyard. It was a beautiful early spring afternoon and the weeping cherry tree in the centre of the graveyard was a veritable bower of blossoms.

He was sitting under the tree beside a neat, well-kept grave when Father John found him.

"Tom, I presume?" the elderly priest said, shaking his hand. "Welcome to Tungold. You've found a nice spot here. Not a bad place to rest for eternity, is it?"

Tom looked down at the grave under the cherry tree. "Jane Elizabeth Adams," he read. "Beloved sister of Lottie. Departed this life aged 96 years. That's quite an innings."

"She was quite a lady," Father John said. "Only passed away last year. She was a pillar of Tungold society. A...what's the word? A philanthropist. Came into some money in her twenties but gave most of it away. You'll see her name all over town. She built the new hall, repaired the church and extended the school, among other things. In fact, she made history. She was the first lady mayor of this region, back in the thirties. And all while caring for an invalid sister."

"She never married?" Tom asked. "Forgive my interest; I like to dabble in writing and I'm always fascinated by eccentric characters."

"Never in the time I knew her," Father John said. "I believe she was widowed young, but I never asked her about it. She didn't like to talk much about her past. As for eccentric, she was sharp as a tack right to the end. Although she did have a few quirks." He scratched his beard, chuckling.

"She always told a story about a ghost train. It runs along here at night, she said. She was convinced it carried the souls of those bound for hell."

AUTHOR'S NOTE

Although I've tried to maintain historical accuracy where possible, I have taken certain liberties. Abortion did not become illegal in New South Wales until 1900, when it was enshrined in the state's *Crimes Act*–although Australian anti-abortion laws were primarily based on the 1861 English *Offences Against the Person Act*.

Railway widows were often given jobs as level crossing gatekeepers in rural Australia–although on average they were a fair bit older than Jane–and there's a wealth of information about the colonial railway system available online and through organisations like the New South Wales Rail Museum. Tungold is fictional, but Goulburn and Berrima are real, and remain beautifully preserved examples of Australian colonial towns.

The Bargo Brush is also real, and was notorious in the early part of the nineteenth century for harbouring 'bolters'–escaped convicts who had become bushrangers. The bushranger era, which reached its peak during the 1850s and 1860s gold rush days, was all but over by the time of *The Iron Line*–it's generally seen to have ended with Ned Kelly's capture and execution in 1880—but I've revived it in the interests of the story. The reference to Captain Starlight is a tribute to the fictional bushranger antihero of Rolf Boldrewood's 1888 novel *Robbery Under Arms*, which is considered one of the classics of Australian colonial literature.

If you enjoyed this book, it would mean a great deal to me if you would consider leaving a review on Goodreads or your online retailer of choice. I always love to hear from readers, so please contact me via my website if you've got something you'd like to share.

I also have a free short story available exclusively to subscribers of my Author Update newsletter, and you'll also be kept in the loop about new releases, giveaways, talks, workshops and other news. You can sign up at www.lmmerrington.com.

ACKNOWLEDGEMENTS

Ask any writer and they'll tell you that it's impossible to produce a book alone. A great many people contributed to this book in its various incarnations.

First, I'd like to thank my wonderful husband, Tristan, who is always there to commiserate and celebrate, and who generously serves as my sounding-board on everything from rudimentary ideas to first drafts to cover design. His support is what has enabled me to go from being someone who writes to being a published author.

My friends and artistic collaborators from the Sydney Artists Retreat were some the first people to get a glimpse of *The Iron Line* in its earliest form, and their enthusiasm and encouragement helped me to keep going.

The volunteer staff at the Goulburn Rail Heritage Centre were very generous with their time and knowledge, and answered all my questions about steam trains and historical railways, no matter how silly. The New South Wales Rail Museum at Thirlmere was another fantastic source of research and inspiration, and where I first learned about widowed level crossing gatekeepers. Thirlmere station, which has been restored to its original glory, also served as aesthetic inspiration for Tungold's counterpart, although it's rather less weather-beaten. I've tried to keep the descriptions of railway operations as accurate as possible, and any errors are mine alone.

I'm very lucky to have a fabulous team of beta readers, who generously gave their time to read an early draft of the manuscript. Katrina Breuker, Catriona Bryce, Paula Hanasz and Chris Millgate-Smith provided honest, constructive and considered feedback, which was invaluable to improving the book.

The Freelance Jungle and Clean Indie Reads Facebook groups also deserve a mention for being major factors in keeping me sane, as well as for offering invaluable advice on the huge learning curves of running a business and developing as an author.

Raewyn Brack worked very patiently with me to come up with a cover that was just right, and Susan Cutsforth provided an editor's eye at a point where I could no longer tell if the book was any good. Any remaining mistakes are all mine.

Last, but definitely not least, I'd like to thank everyone who has supported me on my writing journey so far, especially my parents, friends, and of course my readers. The transition between first and second books turned out to be more difficult than I'd anticipated, and it's been hugely gratifying to receive support from so many quarters, especially those who have taken the time to review *Greythorne*, interview me, engage with my Facebook page, or subscribe to my mailing list. I'd also particularly like to thank the teachers at the two high schools that currently have *Greythorne* on their reading lists for supporting an emerging local author, and the libraries, conferences and festivals in Australia and overseas that have given me the opportunity to connect directly with readers—because an author without readers is just a diarist.